Burning Boats

Zaynab Dawood

THE ISLAMIC FOUNDATON

ISBN: 978-0-86037-477-0

MUSLIM CHILDREN'S LIBRARY

Burning Boats
Author Zaynab Dawood
Editor Farah Alvi
Cover Illustration Kulthum Burgess
Cover/Book Design Nasir Cadir
Coordinator Anwar Cara

Published by
THE ISLAMIC FOUNDATION,
Markfield Conference Centre, Ratby Lane, Markfield,
Leicestershire, LE67 9SY, United Kingdom
Website: www.islamic-foundation.com

QURAN HOUSE, P.O. Box 30611, Nairobi, Kenya

P.M.B. 3193, Kano, Nigeria

All enquiries to
Kube Publishing
Tel: +44(0)1530 249230, Fax +44(0)1530 249656
Email: info@kubepublishing.com
www.kubepublishing.com

A catalogue record of this book is available from British Library

Printed by: Imak Ofset - Turkey

Dedication

For my father and mother.

$\mathcal{A}$cknowledgements

I would like to thank Farah Alvi and everyone at Kube publishing for their support. I would also like to thank Omar Muhammad and Anwar Cara for their useful advice. Most of all I would like to acknowledge the unwavering support, encouragement and help from my husband Abu Abdullah.

Contents

CHAPTER ONE

Changes

THE light from the moon was enough for these men to carry out this sinister undertaking, any more light and maybe someone would see them, and halt the execution of their ominous plot. But there was no one. Just the three of them, moving cautiously, nervously. There was not a single soul around to delay or even stop their treacherous actions. If they saw a pair of eyes watching them, spying through the deep darkness that surrounded them, maybe that would have stopped them. But they continued. In their hearts they knew it was wrong but weakness had overcome them, like so many others in this place.

With the setting of the sun darkness cloaked the village. It was almost quiet except for the small creatures scuttling in the undergrowth, and the occasional braying of a donkey. There was the faint humming and buzzing of insects, the bellows from the buffalo and of course, the night call from the peculiar cockerel. It was nearly midnight and most people were asleep except Ibrahim Ahmed.

He lit a small lantern on his desk; the warm glow cast long shadows that entwined with his brooding thoughts. He walked toward the window, brushed the curtain aside and looked at the sleeping village. It appeared calm and beautiful in the silvery light of the moon. In the distance, lights flickered in the big house on the hill. The sight of which made Ibrahim edgy and he drew the curtains. *There is too much treachery, too much deceit...something has to change.* His thoughts were private but he was certain that others, especially his friends, thought the same. *If something doesn't change, something is going to snap.* He was a resilient man, he thought, but could he save his family from the gathering danger that was unravelling in the village? *Something must be done and quickly...Insha' Allah tomorrow I'll tell the others.* He reassured himself. He blew out the flame and left the room.

The emerging light of dawn lit up the village of Tobay and its people began to stir to life. The women lit the fires in the yards to make ready for the simple breakfast meal. The smoke from the fires mingled with the morning mist and together they conjured the peculiar perfume of the simple hamlet. The daily ritual of the living of life had begun once again. Children emerged dreamy-eyed from their cots. Fathers recounted their day's work in their minds. The coastal hamlet had a fishing harbour, resting on a small bay of mile upon mile of tropical coastland. It was a modest settlement but it could always rely on the harvest that the turquoise seas yielded. The village had more than fifty homes, with white-washed walls and wooden doors, carved with intricate patterns, weathered by the tropical climate and humidity. Scattered between fields were such houses, many were simple and modest structures and others larger and more affluent, which would cast huge shadows over the fields. Small groups of grey buffalo wandered here and there, and scores of dreadful vultures and scavenging sea birds hovered over the harbour. The mosquitoes were everywhere and inescapable.

The morning freshness gave Ibrahim a new confidence. He needed it, especially today, as he would tell the others about his decision. Ibrahim, an upright and thoughtful man, is the village school head teacher. His warmth and wisdom had touched many, from grandparents to children. There was no doubt in people's minds that he was a very special man, but to some folk his principled stance lead to many a serious consequence.

Ibrahim was ready to leave for work. His white garment hung loosely on his slender body and underneath it he wore matching white trousers, which were cotton and baggy, essential in this hot climate. His ebony hair was combed back, speckled with strands of grey. On his face his wheat-coloured skin had now become a rich tan colour with a few wrinkles that were emerging prematurely. His small beard encased his chiselled jaw line and chin. Years of study and more recently hours of insomnia, which were riddled with restless worry, reduced the brightness of his eyes that had once gleamed. A worn-out grey crochet cap covered his head. He carried a worn-out leather satchel in one hand and under his other arm he carried bundled books of various sizes.

"I'm going Zaynab, *assalamu'alaykum*," he called out to his wife.

"*Wa'alaykum as-salam*, but I don't think Umer is ready," she replied.

Umer called out from somewhere in the house, "Abu! Abu! Please wait!"

"I don't want to be late. Your sister has been waiting too!" his father said.

"Waiting for ages!" voiced a young girl.

Umer appeared. He had a mischievous yet innocent expression.

"Son, you're obviously not ready. You'd better come with your sister and the others. Hurry up!" Ibrahim patted his son's head and then walked out onto the veranda. He nodded at Zaynab.

"Please be careful," she remarked. "Don't tell everyone;" her words carried a little fear. She did not want him to become embroiled but at the same time was not entirely happy with his decision either.

"Allah will protect me." The sound of his voice was faint as he turned around the neighbour's house and walked out of sight.

Ayesha sat crossed-legged on a stool on the corner on the veranda, with a large satchel on her lap. She sat there, with dismay at her brother's delay clearly showing on her face. She is a clever and meticulous little girl, not one that should be made to wait. She made tapping noises as she swung her legs under the stool.

"Patience, my dear," called out her mother who was tired of this frequent situation. Umer and his friends had been playing too many games the night before, which was why he was late this morning. Umer emerged on the veranda, ready and looking smart as usual.

"Come on little sister, let's call for Hassan and Fatima," he ordered, avoiding his younger sister's frown.

"You always make me late!" She stomped off behind him.

Voices, loud and disturbed came from the school. A man rushed out.

"O Ibrahim! It's happened again!"

"*Assalamu'alaykum* brother Hamza," Ibrahim said gently and cautiously. He put his arm around Hamza and he ushered him into the school and closed the school doors as passers-by watched the commotion with curiosity.

"It's terrible! Next time someone could get killed!" Hamza fumed with anger.

"Seek refuge in Allah and calm down my friend." Ibrahim turned to his side and looked at his other friend, "Zaid, another sabotage?" Zaid was much calmer than his friend but he too wanted to vent his rage.

"Yes, another boat has been sabotaged. Luckily Khalil's elder sons escaped but the damage is irreparable." Ibrahim sat down and tapped his fingers on the desk. More men entered the school office. More prying villagers hung around in the yard with their children.

"School time soon. Zaid, tell everyone to be careful and perhaps the fishermen shouldn't fish for a few days." This was Ibrahim's attempt to calm the angry men and offer a temporary solution. Pressure had been mounting on the village's fishermen and the situation appeared to have reached boiling point with news of this latest sabotage.

"Ibrahim! How can poorer families cope if they don't work in the harbour?" Hamza's interruption was justified. The men surrounded the school teacher. The proximity gave license to vexatious and unappeasable anger. Hamza shook his head and waved his arms in protest. These men had for so long suppressed their true feelings toward the person responsible for such crimes.

"That's true! Abbas and his friends will bring more fancy boats and fill the harbour, and completely shove the weak ones out." Zaid had too much hatred for Abbas, the richest man in the village. Ibrahim had to quickly vanquish the invisible but almost tangible virulence that streamed out of these men; from their sharp eyes and frowning faces; from their clenched fists and tensed muscles. He put his hand on Zaid's shoulder, firmly. Everyone paused and saw Ibrahim's soothing smile.

"My brother we should be careful which words we use. You know that using foul language is not the way of the believers no matter what the situation." Ibrahim had to guide his friends, he knew better. "All this anger festering inside will destroy our minds and weaken our *imaan*. Turn to Allah, always."

His friends knew they were too hasty and so they sought comfort from his words. Ibrahim sat down beside his desk and this mundane action diffused the tension in the room. Some men found seats, others leaned against the walls. Ibrahim had placated the situated but only fleetingly.

"Come here after *Asr prayer*, I have something very important to say. But keep it quiet." Ibrahim opened the door to let his puzzled friends out and inquisitive parents in.

⚜

"Umer! Umer! Did you hear what happened last night?" Fatima jumped around like an excited mongoose, flapping her dangly arms about.

"Oh! How many times do I have to tell you? *Assalamu' alaykum*. You are definitely a strange girl," laughed Umer, showing off his superiority, after all he was the head teacher's son.

"Listen; really, Hassan's older brothers were injured."

"Fatima, Hassan will tell me himself. Let's collect Maryam first or else we'll be late for school." Umer worried about the time; the reprimand was always more severe for the head teacher's son.

It was an unlikely friendship that kindled from the children's mother's friendship. Fatima lived in the poorer part of Tobay whereas most of her friends lived in what she classed as 'real' homes. Her flippant speech and tactless behaviour was not an indication of her background but rather of her own unique character. Nevertheless all the children were oblivious to the disproportionate endowments of fate. These children made their own little group. There was Umer, who was the natural leader among them. He was shadowed by his closest friend Hassan. Ayesha, for most of her short life had tagged along with her brother who had the burden of not letting her out of his sight. Amongst Ayesha's close friends was Fatima. There was also the polite Maryam, whose little sister, Hafsa, would also tag along. This cluster had two other members, Safiya and Bilal, who unfortunately could not always join them on their playful excursions due to their over protective parents.

The children ran down the paths and jumped over rocks and bushes. In the spirit of childish zest they made faces at each other, a normality especially when they played games. Pausing outside Maryam's home, Umer sensed some kind of disruption.

There is no power or strength except by the will of Allah, he murmured to himself.

He grabbed Fatima's bag and pulled her behind the strong wooden gate. Ayesha perched behind her brother. Peering through the prickly bushes they could see Maryam's father arguing with a man.

"I wonder what is going on?" enquired the skinny and malnourished Fatima.

"Perhaps if you kept quiet and stopped fidgeting like aunty Jameela's mad cockerel, I might find out!"

He glanced at the upper terrace, Maryam waved gingerly through the masses of purple bougainvillea that decorated the northern side of the house.

"She's got a lovely house *Masha' Allah*," whispered Fatima, comparing it to her own little shack.

"Yes, and so have you. Now hush so I can hear." Umer was actually thirteen years old but Allah had blessed him with maturity, something he obviously inherited from his parents. Tension rose in the conversation on the veranda.

"Don't intimidate me! And get off my property!" Maryam's father spoke so loudly that the other children gathered around Umer and Fatima, and some of the neighbours halted their morning chores to witness the racket.

"Move, quick!" Umer ordered his classmates. The angry man left Maryam's home and her father retreated. Away from the scene the schoolchildren tidied their clothes. Some cringed when they saw that their clothes had been stained with mud and grass. Frantically they began to rub off the dirt - a sign of their curiosity. Umer scanned the faces of both men. Apart from anger he couldn't notice anything else. Umer knew uncle Abdullah very well but the other man was unknown, not an inhabitant of Tobay.

A woman's voice penetrated the unease. Abdullah made a noisy entrance to his home: the slamming of doors was to ward off everyone not just his unwelcomed visitor.

"*Abu, Ummi*, I'm going to be late for school." Maryam wanted to leave the house quickly, the tension was becoming unbearable.

"Yes dear, go. *Assalamu'alaykum*, and tell those friends of yours not to be so nosey again." Her mother kissed

Maryam's forehead and straightened her *hijaab*. "Off you go."

"*Assalamu'alaykum* Fatima, Ayesha, Umer." Though Maryam was glad to be on her way to school, she was a little embarrassed by the incident too. Her cheeks were blemished and her thoughts about her father's argument left her while she took on the intrusive inquisition of Fatima.

"What's going on?" Hassan joined his friends.

"You can tell us," probed Umer.

The children spent the next ten minutes on the way to school, exercising their naïve wisdom as they tried to decipher what was going on in their village that was once so peaceful.

CHAPTER TWO

Strange Sky

MIDDAY brought its usual mixture of flies and heat, and not forgetting of course those unwelcome mosquitoes. With tireless dedication and skill, the children would swat any living insect that dared to touch them as they sat behind their small school desks. The school had three classrooms with the simplest of furniture. The vibrancy and charisma of the teachers gave the school light and direction. Umer's teacher, whom they called Madame, skimmed over her pupils. The turnout was not good today, this was always the case when any of the children's father's boats had been set alight the night before. Some parents kept their children at home out of fear and the stronger boys often had to give up school for a week or even a fortnight to help mend their father's boats, or work in the nearby city or town selling roasted nuts and peas, to help feed their families.

Madame never thought that teaching would be so difficult and demanding on the human spirit but like others she kept going, and when some children could not afford their own pencils and books, she provided them. Madame, like most of the mothers in the village, had so much to offer and so many ideas but poverty and lack of security meant their aspirations went unfulfilled.

"Why haven't Bilal and Safiya come to school?" whispered Umer, dodging the teacher's frequent glare.

"Uncle Zaid thinks it's too dangerous." Hassan spoke with seriousness.

"Why? They don't use the boats do they?"

"Umer, we all play in the harbour and that's why they can't play out any more."

It had become a habit for the children to play in every interesting place in the village, especially the harbour. The teacher looked at the boys but not to chastise them for their whispering, rather to know what was going on.

"Maybe we shouldn't play there," Umer calculated.

"It's alright; anyway we play there during the day. The dodgy stuff happens at night." Hassan reasoned with his friend as he enjoyed the games so much he could not bear to abandon them.

"I guess so." Umer enjoyed the games too.

"Right that's enough!" Madame stood up and walked around the classroom. The boys put their heads down and Umer began to write as fast as he could. Hassan looked at the mysterious letters Madame had written in his book. He could not read.

The door opened. Ibrahim walked in. The children gave smiles but maintained the silence.

"*Assalamu'alaykum* children," said Ibrahim.

"*Wa'alaykum as-salam*," they chorused in return.

His eyes scanned the number of heads and noticed that his friend's children were missing. The absence of Zaid's children puzzled him. The class teacher approached Ibrahim. She kept her voice low.

"The problems at the harbour are affecting the children."
She felt a great sense of protection for them. "You should
tell all the children, or at least their parents, that the
harbour and the beach are out of bounds. Anything can
happen, Allah forbid." Ibrahim was very approachable as
a head teacher as well as a member of the community. He
knew very well that Madame and other women, including
his wife, had the resolve to try to change things. This he
admired but when human life was at stake he could not
bear to take risks.

Ibrahim nodded. "Don't worry," he said.

He left the room and the children resumed their
whispering. As he walked out of the stuffy classroom he
knew that he couldn't help those poor fishermen but he
couldn't watch their plight either.

"*Allahu Akbar, Allahu Akbar,*" the call to prayer echoed
from the distant shabby minaret. This small dilapidated
masjid was in serious need of attention. Dozens of men made
their way to *Zuhr* prayer, the rest of the village continued
with its hustle and bustle. Ibrahim noticed the sky as he
left the school. Though it was still very hot, and normal
for this time of the day, the sky looked strange. Clouds, in
mysterious shapes, appeared to dance about in the sky.

"*Assalamu'alaykum.* I came to collect you. I thought we'd
go to the *masjid* together." Abdullah, Maryam's father, had
a strong and fine composure and his voice was always clear
and confident.

"*Wa'alaykum as-salam*, Abdullah. You know about the
meeting?"

"Yes, Khalil told me. What happened last night is
horrendous and one of Abbas's men came to me this
morning, urging me to sell my land. I put him straight."

Abdullah frowned when he spoke as he too loathed those wicked men.

"The sky is changing. Allah protect us," said Ibrahim as he walked ahead leaving his confused friend behind.

Instead of listening to me, he's concerned about the sky. What's happening in this village? thought Abdullah.

Abdullah and Ibrahim had shared much of their lives together. Their childhood was spent in Tobay after which their parents sent them to the city when they were young men, to institutions where education was regarded as higher and more esteemed. For a few years their lives took different courses. Abdullah explored trade in the province with his wealthy father while Ibrahim took the post of a teacher at a less affluent school in the city. Circumstances drew them back to the village and their friendship was rekindled.

On top of the hill, grey mist enveloped Abbas's house. It was the largest and most extravagant house in the village. Inside, words were being exchanged with anger and recrimination.

"What do you mean he didn't listen? Everyone listens to me!" Abbas slammed his clenched fist on the table. The man standing in front of him cowered. Another equally ugly man interrupted.

"Mr Abbas, we know that you are the wealthiest man in the village, probably one of the wealthiest in the province but Abdullah is wealthy too. If he doesn't want to sell his land, there's nothing we can do. He doesn't own any boats for us to destroy." This man though as bad as the others, wanted to convey to his domineering boss that enough was enough. Abbas, a stockily built man with a peculiarly small head and hooked nose, rather like a vulture, knew exactly what his underling was saying.

"Sit down, all of you please." Abbas tried the calmer approach. "Listen carefully, I don't do what I do to gain more wealth. Of course that's one thing I get, but these people are less advantaged than myself. It is obvious that I have power in the village and I know what is best for this poor lot." In reality it seemed that he enjoyed playing games of power and control. His sly smile pervaded the room. His henchmen responded accordingly.

"My boats are petrol powered, can get further out at sea quicker and carry bigger nets. These low people don't understand that their shabby, pathetic handmade boats are ruining this village. As a people we need to go further and only I can take them there." He stood up and walked towards a large polished cabinet, took out a key from his waistcoat and unlocked the door. As ever he took out a small bag and locked the door again. "Here." He placed the bag on the grey marble table. "I appreciate your efforts. Consider this a bonus for your hard work on that Khalil's boat. Now, you may leave."

The men marched out of the room, each one thinking of his bonus. First it was coins that had clanked on the marble table now they received notes. Old, creased and musty notes that had passed from fair traders into the hands of cunning men. These men had families and wanted to free themselves from the suffocation of poverty. Abbas gave them a chance for a different life, a life where they could frequently hold bundles of old notes. For some the origins of such notes did not disturb them but a few men did question their master about it. They received physical injuries as an answer.

"And remember, I want Abdullah's land," ordered Abbas. This man was ruthless and no amount of harm to any person or property could dampen the pursuit of his selfish designs.

This was Abbas's life. He knew nothing else. As a child he was an amiable boy but when he was a young man his parents died and he inherited wealth that would provide a secure future. In contrast, however, he made a living out of taking away the security of others. The need he felt for more removed any trace of compassion and love from his heart. His mind was stripped of empathy and consideration for others. Greed had entrenched its power in his blood and its ugliness became his eyes from which he viewed others: below him.

Back at the school the children enjoyed a mid-afternoon break on the playground. It was a simple playground, with two wooden benches, a steel cylinder as a bin and a rectangular white frame protruding out of the ground at the back of the playground, which was used as football goal posts. Behind the school building lay a few feet of compost which was used by the younger children to plant their own vegetables and flowers. Often, nothing grew because of the over-zealousness of the young gardeners. The noise level rose on the dusty playground as the children ran, jumped, fought, fell out and made up during this ten-minute break. Umer and Hassan resumed their naughtiness too.

"Umer is scared!" Hassan teased cruelly. He wanted to squeeze every little doubt about the harbour out of his friend.

"Stop it!" shouted the red-faced Umer. "You know I'm not! And I'm much cleverer than you anyway!" Being the head teacher's son gave him a superiority complex, however false.

"It's strength, wit and courage that is needed not your brains..." Hassan thoroughly enjoyed tormenting his overnice friend. The girls joined in the vicious but innocent game.

"Well my brother can run faster than you, everyone knows that!" said Ayesha defensively, recalling yesterday's race in the field.

"Oh yes, Umer is much faster than you," ribbed Fatima picking up a twig and throwing it at Hassan.

"Well I can swim better than the lot of you!" exclaimed the nearly defeated Hassan holding onto the last piece of dignity he had.

"Ha ha! Hassan is getting upset! Oh brother, now calm down, please. Calm down." Oozing with sarcasm Umer put his arm around his angry friend. Fatima and Ayesha laughed at the boys.

"Now let's see. Are you inviting me to a competition someday? For a race through the lanes? We can't swim because the beach is out of bounds." Umer articulated Hassan's thoughts.

"Of course, but these girls can't come!" Hassan's patience with the girls ended.

"Well I want to watch my brother beat you." Ayesha was as strong-willed as her mother.

"Well, I want to watch my brother, my brother, my brother." Hassan imitated Ayesha's words with disgust. Hassan had three older brothers and no sisters, and he could not fathom a brother and sister relationship at all, especially one which was as close as Ayesha's and Umer's.

"If I had a sister like you, I don't know what I'd do!"

"Hassan, leave her. She's only a kid." Umer was always protective toward his sister, even if she was wrong.

"If you were my brother I would spill a jar of ants on your bed while you were still asleep in it!" Fatima kept laughing while the other children that had gathered there giggled.

"Stop it! We can't race just yet, we have too much school work to get through. Maybe another day." Umer remembered Madame giving them more work than usual. This was her attempt at keeping the children indoors and out of harm's way.

During the entire argument Maryam kept quiet, her mind was filled with worries about the harbour. She imagined her mother and grandmother at home sitting on the veranda preparing vegetables to cook, with long faces. Maryam overheard her father telling them not to leave the house. She rarely saw her father angry. It was because of that man who shouted at her father, she thought. Vaguely she made a mental connection between the man and the harbour but it was short lived.

Fatima tugged at her arm. "Hey, dreamer. Shall we play chase?"

Maryam did not want to play, then she worried about her friend Safiya who was absent from school today. "Safiya and Bilal didn't come to school today. They never miss school."

"Didn't you hear? Mr Zaid is keeping them home until the problems stop. Come and play, Madame will ring the bell soon." Fatima pulled Maryam hard, pulling her out of her dreaming too.

Madame came out and rang the rusty brass bell, then held it and said: "Right children! In you all come, quietly now."

The children lined up and walked in pairs towards the school doors. They all obeyed with the odd pushing and shoving here and there.

Umer whispered to Hassan. "You know you shouldn't behave like that with Ayesha. She's only ten years old. You should treat her like you would your own sister, if you had one."

"I know, I was just about to apologise," Hassan said with embarrassment yet feeling real admiration for his intelligent friend.

"Yes, but I thought I'd say it for you!" Looking at each other the boys laughed.

Inside, Ibrahim sat quietly in his office. Feeling weak he put his hands together to make *dua*. Humbled before his Lord, tears fell from his eyes. "All praise is to You, You are the Kind the Merciful. O Allah, there is so much trouble in this little village, so please save us from it and let us all be good to each other."

The door opened and his wife walked in. "Ibrahim, I have brought your lunch." She placed the parcel on his desk. "Eat well. I'm sure your meeting will be a long one." With deliberate care she unwrapped the parcel so the food was ready to eat.

"*Jazak Allah*, Zaynab. Yes, it probably will be long. Please make *dua* for me."

"Of course." Zaynab had a modest and kind temperament and her love for Allah and her constant goodness made her a very special lady. Leaving the office she turned and looked at her husband. Her words were comforting, "You are a man of knowledge and faith. When we moved to this village it was because this village needed a teacher and people ridiculed your knowledge. Remember? They said you could earn more as a fisherman than as a teacher. You persevered and in the last ten years the school has flourished."

"Times have changed. I have many friends here now but I don't want to live in a dangerous place." Ibrahim sensed the extreme danger. Things were already getting out of hand and so he had decided to move away to a place where work and accommodation would be easily available.

Zaynab persisted. "Allah brought you here for a good purpose. Don't let yourself be driven out by thugs. We teach our Umer and Ayesha not to give into bad things, so why should we? Because Abbas is rich and powerful? He thinks he's got power but Allah is the One Who has power. If you decide that we should leave, let it be for a better reason. I don't want you to give in to that man. I don't want him to think you're weak and running away."

She stood beside the bookcase, her height nearly matching it. She wiped a few beads of perspiration off her forehead with a corner of her long printed shawl. Neither of them felt intimidated or scared by Abbas's tricks but she too could not bear seeing others hurt by him. Very occasionally, when their paths would cross, she would advocate the villagers' rights in a polite tone but her husband's silence had the greatest effect on Abbas. She opened the door.

"I must go now. By the way, have you noticed it's eerie outside? Something strange is in the air." She left the school and headed back home.

Her words carried so much weight that Ibrahim couldn't eat his food properly. Soon it would be time for *Asr* prayer and the meeting. Feeling anxious, Ibrahim paced up and down his office. "*Allah* suffices and is the Best Disposer of affairs", he recited this repeatedly to give himself strength. A few minutes passed and Ibrahim felt rejuvenated. He looked around the room and decided to tidy up a little, ready for the meeting.

Chairs in place and room clean, he was ready to enjoy his meal, although it had gone cold. As he ate his bread, he could hear men gathering outside. It was time to tell the others, no matter how hard it was going to be as he knew very well what his friends' reactions would be.

The men gathered outside the school office. Abdullah's crisp and fresh attire made him stand out from his peers. Khalil's worn-out clothes reflected his life as a fisherman and his rough skin was a testament to his toil in the merciless elements. Zaid paced around his friends. He was a man who was always troubled by something and his frown and grimace intensified or faded with the seriousness of his problems. His dark skin glowed in the heat and his fingers hardly left the small bald patch that was appearing at the top of his head. He rubbed and massaged it, a habit which helped him think, but unearthed other problems too. Hamza's fleshy belly was the first thing everyone noticed when they saw him, especially with his limited height.

"Khalil, you were very fortunate. Allah saved your sons," uttered Abdullah, who did not want to disclose his previous argument with Abbas's right-hand man.

"Yes, very fortunate but things need to change," Khalil spoke firmly. "They have threatened to burn our homes next!"

"Gentlemen, let's keep our comments quiet, the children will be leaving school shortly and we don't want their mothers to find out what's happening," said Zaid.

Zaid motioned towards the playground where some mothers had already began their speculation and whispering.

"It's a little humid, don't you think? The animals are behaving awkwardly too," said Hamza, who owned a few goats, chickens and a noisy cockerel.

Exchanging idle chatter, the men waited for Ibrahim.

Dozens of children escaped from the classrooms and poured out into the playground. It was a small school, with a handful of teachers and the building itself was rather dilapidated. The parents admired the dedication of the head teacher, who was often spotted either retiling on the rooftop or fixing the rusty iron gate. Resources in the classroom were scarce and the teachers were expected to do more than classroom duties. This was never a problem. Every teacher, including the head teacher had vision and commitment for the school.

"Who else has yet to arrive?" questioned Hamza, the village shopkeeper, as he counted heads as if he was counting sacks of rice.

The office door opened. *"Assalamu'alaykum* brothers. Come in." Ibrahim avoided making eye contact. "I cannot thank Allah enough for giving me good company like yourselves."

The men were seated around the room except the host who marched in front of the window.

"With much thought and *dua* I've decided to..." and he paused and cleared his throat "to leave the village and move to another..."

The men interrupted his words. "What do you mean? You can't go!" Hamza raised his voice again.

Zaid's voice was louder, "Ibrahim, don't give in to that man. We must do something together!" Zaid resumed scratching his bald spot.

Abdullah's voice rose above the clamour. "We can't give in to that man. Ibrahim you have taught us so much about truth and dignity and now you want to abandon us?" Abdullah implored, firm in his resolve.

Ibrahim sat behind his desk. "Please let me finish. Please?" His calm demeanour was not shaken in the least. "You may think that I am running away but I am not. Allah knows my intention. The world is filled with problems and every town and village has its share of bad people."

Never until now had his friends become impatient with Ibrahim's words. Looking at one another, the men shook their heads in disbelief. Acknowledging their dismay, Ibrahim silently asked Allah to put eloquence in his speech. He remembered the words of Prophet Musa, *"Oh my Lord! Expand me my breast, ease my task for me and remove the impediment from my speech, so they may understand what I say"*.

Abdullah stood up. He wasn't angry, in fact he felt sorry for his close friend. Abdullah's tall and broad body dominated the small space between the men and the head teacher's desk. Some thought that Ibrahim was *running away* but his closest friend knew otherwise. Such indignity was beyond Ibrahim. What was really happening was Ibrahim's recognition that he was helpless against a force where his words and kindness could not conquer. Abdullah felt the same. As a man with wealth and some influence in the region he could not defeat Abbas or even stage an opposition equal in might and fear. Abbas's game was new and his tactics were beyond the mental, psychological and even physical strength of these men. Despite this something churned in these men and it would only be a matter of time and unforeseeable events that would animate this dormancy and bring about Abbas's downfall.

"Ibrahim, our brother! So many people have been hurt, betrayed and nearly killed because of that man. And every time, most people have fallen apart. But Allah gave you knowledge and wisdom and through your advice, people have been stronger. *Al-Hamdulillah* for the strength Allah has given us, but the time has come not for you to leave but for all of us to take action against that man and we can only do it with your help." Abdullah returned to his seat, hot and red-faced.

The shopkeeper spoke. "Yes something needs to be done. I think we should contact the police from the city."

"Don't you remember," reminded Khalil, "Abbas threatened anyone who dared to contact the police?" Threats to his livelihood was enough of a problem but threats to his family kept him back. A threat to his life angered him but threats to his family scared him. The adrenalin rush he experienced on severe waves as he pulled heavy nets with other fishermen could not match in potency the fear he had for his family.

Hamza continued, he was known to be a quiet man but now his sense of justice over-powered his placid nature. "What can Abbas do that he isn't doing already? Do you know how many poor people have debt accounts with me? It's difficult to see them suffering, they don't have a coin to spend on a bar of soap. Every week they say that they are trying to fix their boats. Only for them to be ruined again. The accounts are getting so big that I won't be able to buy new stock next month if debts are not repaid. Please don't think that I am saying all this for my benefit. I can see the indignity and sadness in these people's eyes when they leave my shop with their skinny kids screaming for candy."

All the men nodded, even Ibrahim. They were all surprised at Hamza's situation. Hamza who no longer felt like a small insignificant figure, spoke again with fiery determination. "If you decide to leave, I pray Allah helps me, because I'm going to go to the police, even if I go on my own."

The men were amazed at Hamza's words, and a few of them were quietly impressed.

Although the meeting was arranged so that Ibrahim could take a load off his chest, it appeared to be the ideal forum for all the men to discuss events together. As Ibrahim watched the men discussing these matters, he noticed that the *imam* wasn't there.

"Hold on, anyone know where Imam Abdur-Rahman is?" His absence disturbed him, the *imam* was a very special friend. Now the men noticed too.

Zaid, fed up with all the talk, made a flippant comment, "Well, he's probably painting the *masjid*!"

"Oh please Zaid! The *imam* puts a lot of hard work into that *masjid*." Abdullah put his friend straight. The village *masjid* was in a shameful state with its broken tiles and cracked walls. Even its minaret was propped up by coconut tree trunks. The *imam* was actually from a neighbouring village, two miles south of Tobay. Abdur-Rahman, a devout young man, never minded the daily trips, sometimes by horse and cart and other times on foot.

Zaid walked over to the window. "It's unusually dark, don't you think? I'm sure there's an hour or so to *Maghrib*." He was quite perplexed by the darkening sky. Zaid took his sight off the sky for a moment and looked into the yard. A dubious figure ducked behind a wall. A trace of suspicion flickered in Zaid's heart, "*I seek refuge with Allah*," he repeated to himself.

"*Assalamu'alaykum* dear friends. Sorry for the delay. I just had to arrange transport early for tonight. Weather doesn't look too good. Ibrahim, can you lead *Isha* tonight?" The *imam* was totally oblivious; he hadn't an inkling of the tension in the room. He sat on the chair pushed towards him. "Have I missed much?"

Zaid walked over to the *imam* and whispered in his ear, "Imam, were you followed here?"

"Maybe," the *imam* whispered with a serious expression. Raising his voice he said, "This meeting should end now. I think I was being followed, though no danger came to me, *Al-Hamdulillah*."

All the men stood up, each suspecting that a spy had been sent by Abbas. It was amazing how information reached Abbas.

Ibrahim became anxious. "Yes, I think it's too dangerous to continue now. We don't want any more problems tonight at the harbour. I'll speak to the *imam* tomorrow." Ibrahim and the *imam* exchanged glances.

"I'm certain I saw someone lurking outside in the yard." Zaid compounded everyone's unease.

"Don't worry, Allah will protect us." The *imam's* voice was strong and comforting. The men were just about to leave but Ibrahim knew he had to finish.

"My friends, I shall be leaving by the end of next month. That is my final decision." All the men were taken aback. They could not believe what they had heard. "You are more than welcome to join me or visit me anytime."

So Ibrahim managed to say what he had intended. His final words were, for some, a glimmer of hope for themselves, as their home village no longer had the security and goodness it once had. And for others Ibrahim's words threw them further into hopelessness and dread.

Except for Ibrahim, all the men left silently without saying a word to anyone. Their outlines silhouetted against the partially iridescent sky. In the sky above, dark murky clouds lingered from the afternoon. Standing in the doorway Ibrahim looked at the village. The village was quietening: on one side, men pushed carts carrying fodder up the hills towards their homes; in the fields the farm boys rounded up the sheep and goats; in the lane heading out of the village, a man holding a long stick, walked behind a small herd of buffalo; and just below the huge house on the hill, near the tamarind groves, a cluster of gluttonous vultures perched, ripping, tearing and eating a dead buffalo. The stone-paved pathway leading to the *masjid* was narrow and shrouded by small shrubs. The band of men moved sombrely upon it, like the tired grey buffalo. Ibrahim locked the school office door and then the gate and headed for the *masjid*. Questions assailed his conscience. *Did you do the right thing? Are your intentions pure? Why are you really leaving?* But he knew and Allah knew too. He needed to break away from the fetters before they tightened. To him there appeared to be an unjust hierarchy. An oppressive king with a large palace and servile villagers, working day after day, ruthlessly exploited, like those poor grey buffalo. Ibrahim hated the way most people submitted to that proud and greedy king. He wondered whether he should have such negative thoughts about Abbas, but then it's the vulture that makes a feast of the buffalo carcass. His judgement was sound. He abandoned such thoughts and began his *dhikr* as he neared the *masjid*. "Truly in the remembrance of Allah do hearts find tranquillity".

Whilst the men were burdened with difficult thoughts and heavy emotions, the boys of the village were preparing for *salah*. Some wore white crochet hats, others wore different coloured cotton hats, and some did not wear hats. Hassan stood under a huge tree, straightening his crumpled clothes. His family did not own an iron or any other electrical instrument; they couldn't afford it and the electric cables did not extend to their homes.

"Hassan, *assalamu'alaykum*. Come on, let's go for *salah*," called out Umer.

"*Wa'alaykum as-salaam*. Should we call for Bilal on the way?" Hassan really wanted to know why Bilal had been absent from school.

"Yes, let's go." Umer was a natural leader, especially for boys like Hassan.

They walked in the opposite direction to the *masjid*. The odd change in the weather had disturbed all the animals and their owners were finding it hard to control them. A shepherd ushered a small flock of noisy sheep. Hassan could not resist the temptation and ran towards them.

"Hassan, leave those sheep alone. Why do you tease them?" Umer shouted at his mischievous friend.

"Hassan! Hassan! Stop it now! Before I tell your brothers!" shouted the shepherd.

Umer began laughing, he knew something Hassan didn't know.

"My brothers aren't here. I just like to play with animals!" Umer and the shepherd both thought that Hassan was behaving like an animal.

"You're scaring them, and which sensible person plays with sheep?" shouted the shepherd.

"What are you laughing at?" remarked Hassan who sensed trouble was near.

"Oh nothing, you just look like an animal, a sheep ready for *qurbani*!"

Suddenly, Hassan's eldest brother seized Hassan by the shoulders and whisked him out of the way so the shepherd could get past. Hassan took one look at his brother and frowned.

"You need to say something to the shepherd", said his brother.

As usual, he knew what to say: "I'm sorry for being a nuisance." Hassan spoke softly as his brother's grip was so tight he could hardly speak.

The shepherd nodded and walked off. His brother then released him. He gave Hassan a thump on his back, which Hassan's body was so accustomed to that he felt immune to its pain.

"Hassan! You should be like Umer. It's embarrassing to see you make a fool of yourself. You're twelve not three years old."

"I'm sorry."

"We're on our way to get Bilal for *salah*," said Umer wanting to change the subject.

"Hurry up otherwise you'll be late!"

"Why were you laughing?" asked Hassan.

"Because I saw your brother watching and I knew he would sort you out!"

The boys walked down the lane and passed many people as the village was winding down for the evening. Ahead of them they saw Bilal with his sister Safiya, standing at the gate of Maryam's house.

"Are you ready for the *masjid*?" said Umer.

"Yes Umer," called out Bilal. "I just brought my sister here, wait for me." Bilal took his sister inside the garden. "I'll collect you after *Maghrib*," he said and then joined his friends and went to the *masjid*. Bilal had acquired an irritating habit that resembled his father's incessant head-touching, which was to rub the area between his eyebrows. A pink inflamed patch was a reminder to all that he carried a portion of his father's concern for Tobay and its people.

The girls watched the boys. The sight of the boys walking freely and safely in the darkening twilight caught the attention of Maryam and Safiya, who were the same age. They were a little envious of the boys. For the past few years the girls subconsciously felt restrained. They could no longer enjoy the greater freedom they had when they were younger. Most of all, the yearning of the girls to pray salah in the masjid was ignored. Occasionally, they would discuss amongst themselves along with Ayesha and Fatima.

"Sometimes I want to pray in the *masjid*." Maryam was thinking aloud.

"Me too, but they don't have any room for us there," replied Safiya.

"But they have enough room for all the boys!" piped up Maryam.

"It is very small and the *imam* once said that if they ever built a new *masjid* it would be big enough for girls and their mums too," remarked Safiya, positively.

Maryam began to think of her mother, Halima, and what she would say to her whenever she approached the topic: *"Not everyone follows the true teachings of our beloved Prophet..."* she would say. *"He gave us women permission to pray in the masjid but some people frown on women going to the masjid. I've never been inside a masjid, nor your grandmother, not even your aunties. But the world is changing and I'm sure one day you'll be able to pray in the masjid."* Maryam wished things would change now, while she was a ten year old.

"Come on let's play a little before *salah*," said Hafsa, Maryam's younger sister. The trio left such ideas and began their girlish games.

CHAPTER THREE

Typhoon

THE village slept but the night watchers at the harbour were vigilant. Khalil and two other men sat around a small campfire, which crackled and spat every time fresh twigs were thrown in, it's dancing flames flickered in the cold breeze. To the east of the men, a row of dozen wooden boats merged into the darkness and beyond lay a black mass of trees. Further down the creek, the bigger boats stood, making an occasional reflection from their steel sides from the silvery grey moon. And behind them was endless ocean, immense and unfathomable. On this night the ocean was restless. The distant stars could not add any shimmer to the water.

These men had found the courage to camp on the beach in the asphyxiating darkness. The light from the flames illumined their tense faces and eager eyes while their hands grasped their batons with steely grit. They were ready to take on any men sent from Abbas and revenge was burning within them but this was momentarily being quelled by the change in the atmosphere. As the night wore on, light rain began to fall.

"This is strange. It's not the rainy season. We've got months yet." Khalil mentally counted the number of months left for the annual rainy season. The two men stood up and looked up at the sky. Black clouds billowed and filled the sky.

"What's going on?" Khalil could not understand what was taking place.

In Ibrahim's home a few lanterns were lit in the main living area. It was a medium-sized room that was used as a lounge and dining area, and sometimes for sleeping too. On the northern and southern walls were windows with wooden shutters, which were covered with hand-made cotton curtains. There were a few shelves on the wall, holding books and other items. The floor was covered with rugs, large and small of different colours. The house was furnished in an entirely simple and practical manner. These were not a people for undue luxury. There were, however, decent wooden chairs and a strong table, some sort of wall cabinet and some padded stools for the children. Large square cushions were haphazardly placed around the room and Ibrahim's desk was overloaded with *hadith* books and other such material. Nevertheless this room was calm and peaceful, even visitors felt this, perhaps it was from the blessing of all the *dhikr* that was done here.

Zaynab was reading the Qur'an and Ibrahim was sitting on his prayer mat. Both had completed their *tahajjud* prayers. The room filled with the sound of the rain on the roof. Ibrahim looked at his wife. They exchanged knowing glances. They went over to the window. The rain and thunder had disturbed the entire village. Ibrahim wrapped a woven shawl around himself and walked out onto the veranda. The cockerel crowed and noised off in its own particular manner. The cows and buffalo bellowed, donkeys began to bray incessantly, and dogs barked and howled. The sounds got louder, the rain fell harder, and nearly every living creature was awake.

People watched the sky in total bewilderment. Overhead thunder rumbled in the clouds, and the sky was momentarily ripped apart by bolts of lightning. The sky heaved, and then it burst. Torrents of water gushed from the sky, so much so that people could not look up anymore, beneath their feet was water, and more water. In absolute frenzy mothers rushed their children indoors; fathers, men and teenage boys ran out onto the lanes yelling "Typhoon! typhoon!"

Zaynab checked on her children Umer and Ayesha, who were watching in amazement.

"Ummi, what's going on?" Ayesha was quite afraid of what was going on, an expected emotion from a ten-year-old.

"Ayesha dear, it's probably a typhoon."

"But it's not the rainy season yet. How can that be?" Umer was very confused.

"Umer son, everything in the world, takes place because of Allah's plan, not because man has planned. May Allah help us and forgive us. I think it's a typhoon and it's not over yet." Zaynab worried about her friends, especially those in the small feebly built homes. Umer was thinking the same.

"Ummi, what about Fatima's house? And Hassan's? Hassan's father is not even there. He's gone to the harbour." Umer was raising his voice with anxiety.

"Yes Umer. Calm down, we need to go there; your father has gone to check on the school and *masjid*. Oh Allah, please help us! Right! Both of you get dressed, quickly; I can't leave you alone here on a night like this!" Her final command was sharp and loud, as her friend's vulnerability dawned on her.

Fatima and Hassan both lived with their families in shanty dwellings. Zaynab imagined that those homes could not bear the force of the rain and the inevitable landslides. Zaynab ventured into the flood with her son and daughter, who clung on to each other while she led the way. Every few steps she turned back to look at her children, to check if they were behind her. Unwilling to surrender to the might of the rush, she continued, pulling her wet, drenched figure through the torrents, praying that her friends would be unharmed, and that their homes would not be ruined.

People were out on their verandas or in their courtyards, and those with a few animals attempted to calm them and return them back to their shelters at the back of their houses. The muddy hummocks ceded to the pelting rain, so that mounds and small trees were swept away in the cascade. To the east of the village the foothills and slopes groaned with the weight of the downpour, for it was the place where the poor families had made their nests. Somehow these simple homes did not look wretched or squalid because the people who inhabited them had a richness of the heart that even the richest man in the village could not fathom. Allah had blessed them with contentment with their modest provision, and although they were poor they did not feel deprived.

Taking a short-cut to Fatima's house, Zaynab left the lane and began walking on the stony rises leading to the slopes. She held her children's hands and was careful not to fall into the trenches and ditches, which were appearing everywhere. And all the time the relentless rain pelted their faces.

"Ummi…I'm scared." Umer gave into his confusion and shock; the hazard of their plight brought out his vulnerable side. Zaynab did not want to show him her face, totally drenched by the rain. Her eyes were swollen and red from tears. The love for her friends and the danger they may be experiencing was the cause for her weeping, not the force and devastating drive of the rain. Her children would not be able to understand that so she hid her face away, not wanting to reinforce their fears.

"Everything will be fine, *Insha' Allah*. Don't worry children, Allah is with us. "

It didn't look good. Even as they waded through the water Zaynab noticed some of people's belongings floating by. It was dark and visibility was poor but there was enough light to see the ruptured sides on the stronger shacks. There was no sign of Fatima's house. Fatima saw them and ran towards them.

"Aunty Zaynab! Aunty Zaynab!" Sobbing loudly Fatima flung herself onto her beloved aunty and held her tight. Her mother followed suit, holding dripping bundles.

"Our home has collapsed, Zaynab. We came out to look when it started, but the water and mud from the hills washed it away." She spoke quietly, totally shocked by the incident. Zaynab looked up at the hills, she could see a small river running through it and broken branches and twigs had found their way here, shattering their flimsy homes. Zaynab embraced her friend.

"Allah bless you, Ruqaiya. Don't worry; everything will be all right as long as no one is hurt. You will stay with us, come now." Zaynab led the way again. Fatima's father followed shortly. Umer kept thinking of poor Fatima whose house had been washed away. Ayesha was numb with shock, just battling through the village in this state was enough for her.

Holding his cloak above his head Ibrahim made his way to the school. The desolation around him, even in the darkness of the night made him swallow hard and sent an eerie chill down his spine. For unlike the other events, he could not blame this calamity on Abbas. He prayed and asked Allah to help all of them and to stop the rain. Running along the lane, with mud squelching under his shoes, he noticed the *masjid* and how strange it appeared. He paused and stared at it. The rain splattered against his face as he pulled the shawl back. The old *masjid* stood in a bizarre way, illuminated by the occasional shards of lightening and the lanterns burning within it. The trees in the courtyard rocked to and fro with the force of the wind. Debris, clothes and paper tossed by the wind hurled towards its walls. The *masjid* was the source and anchor for all their hope and faith, and now it was being battered by the sudden typhoon. Ibrahim realised what disturbed him. The *masjid* stood crest-fallen, beaten by the relentless rain. The minaret had gone. The unremitting downpour had been too much for the debilitated minaret and so it yielded to its power. It no longer greeted the villagers but now it lay as a pile of muddy rubble, awaiting more destruction from the deluge. "O Allah, please help us. Please...." He ran towards the school, avoiding to register anything around him, dodging any villager who may stop him as his thoughts were with the school, the children's school.

Drenched and sweating, Ibrahim fumbled with the keys, which felt cool against his warm and sticky hands. Amazingly the rain was slowing down. Maybe his *duas* were being answered. "*Al-Hamdulillah*," he reasoned with himself, then he sighed with relief as the torrents eased. As he unlocked the gates Zaid came behind him. Zaid said: "It's bad! I thought it was a typhoon but no..." He was so out of breath he could not complete the sentence. Bewildered and confused the two friends looked at each other.

"I went to check on the *masjid*. I've got an extra set of keys and battery torches." He waved the bright torch in front of Ibrahim who winced from the sudden light.

"Oh sorry! I saw you go past the *masjid* so I followed you." Zaid was a loyal friend, shadowing Ibrahim at every opportunity.

"So you were in the *masjid*?"

"Yes Ibrahim. I lit lanterns and checked everything. The roof is all right, a few broken windows but did you see the minaret? It was going to happen anyway. Poor Imam, having to cope with such a ramshackle place."

Both men walked across the yard, through a stream, which was about a foot deep. The metal bins had overturned and the rubbish was floating in the muddy torrent. The children's small garden was ruined too; Ibrahim frowned when he saw that, he knew the disappointment it would cause the little ones. Something then caught his attention. He walked closer. A small tree had survived. It's thin trunk and branches moved gently in the rain. He smiled when he remembered who planted the tree. Ayesha planted its seed a few years ago. He found it amazing that her tree was the only thing that had not been destroyed.

"It will soon be *Fajr*, so we'll have light," Zaid remarked, thinking how much easier it would be with more light especially now that the electricity cables were down. Ibrahim thought of a different light, the light that would help this village out of this mayhem.

Ibrahim opened the door. Water gushed beneath them, it came from inside the school. With utter dismay Zaid entered.

"Oh no Ibrahim! Where is this water coming from?"

Swallowing his dismay and disappointment Ibrahim went into the school. He knew he should not be overwhelmed by the incident.

"Praise is due to Allah in all circumstances." He pointed his finger to the ceiling where the lights used to be. Instead, all that could be seen was the dark sky with black threatening clouds veiling it.

"The roof has caved in! Oh Allah!" Zaid spoke the obvious.

"Yes, these things do happen. At least no one was in the building." Ibrahim began picking up pieces of rubble and wood, thoughts about rebuilding with no funds whirled in his mind.

"Don't worry Ibrahim," Zaid knew quite well that his friend would not be defeated by this event, "we'll fix the school and *masjid*. Everyone will help out, *Insha' Allah*." Zaid began picking up pieces of soggy wood and other debris, *maybe this will delay Ibrahim's departure, maybe he won't leave us...* Guiltily, Zaid thought how this flood might make Ibrahim stay.

A few miles away, someone else was thinking the same, but with quite different, and perhaps dangerous intentions. In the stormy blackness of this night, Abbas's house made an eerie silhouette; its heavy iron gates loomed impenetrable against the night sky. The imposing walls of the house added to its threatening aspect. No light could be seen from the house except the window through which Abbas watched. From the flickering candles and lanterns burning inside the room, the light wavered from bright yellow to a murky orange, making the window gleam like sparks off a flint. The house stood like a towering shadow on the hill with one burning eye.

With no personal damage or loss to ponder over, Abbas thought about the news he had received in the evening.

"The teacher is going to leave soon. He asked others to join him and someone is going to the police." That was the message from his "worker", who was sent to spy at the meeting.

"Going to leave? The police? Well, what a challenge!" Abbas spoke aloud with deep malice in his voice. There was no one in the room to hear him or to make comments.

"So they want to stand up to me...." He walked around his room, gesticulating with his arms and shoulders. "The teacher wants to leave? Leave this picturesque village!" Ibrahim's intention infuriated him as he enjoyed ridiculing the teacher every time they met; but it was always Ibrahim's dignified silence that angered Abbas more. He walked over to the window again, dawn was approaching but the village was still cast in a misty shroud. The rain was subsiding. *Pity*, Abbas thought, *this typhoon can't have left their homes, or school, or that mosque. There must be some damage.* Peering out of the window, he said to himself: "Surely this event will open doors for me!"

One of his servants stood behind his closed door, so he heard Abbas's last words. This servant had involuntarily served this master for a couple of years now and the extent of his treachery was painfully pricking his conscience; he did not want to work for him, but like so many others, had no other means of livelihood.

Abbas called for him. "Nasser, Nasser. Get here;" that was one of Abbas's polite summons, thought Nasser. Nasser waited a minute, so as not to get caught out for eavesdropping, and then entered the room.

Abbas was seated, on his fine wood and cane chair, his baldhead shining in the candlelight.

"Right Nasser, listen."

Nasser sat on one of the wooden chairs against the wall. "Yes master."

"This typhoon was quite unexpected, quite like Ibrahim's plans but I feel I should take matters more seriously now..."

Nasser became anxious; *more serious, what is he thinking?*

"I'm sure you know that the teacher has a very special place in the hearts of these people....he does influence them and especially those little children of theirs....so your job is to find out what damage has been done, especially to the school and mosque. I'm sure the 'wise, noble, righteous,' teacher won't abandon the village in this crisis....so we should use this time to buy the trust of the people." Abbas looked at Nasser for acknowledgement of his statements but found Nasser looking puzzled.

"Don't you understand? Obviously not!"

"I'm sorry but I don't, why do you want them to "trust" you?"

"Because they are easily influenced by Ibrahim! And if he decides in all his wisdom nonsense that he should leave then half of the village will too! They will leave and who will run the harbour?" By this time Abbas was red with his self-induced rage; beads of sweat covered his head and face, and his veins protruded on his face and neck.

Poor Nasser, he still couldn't grasp the master plan. "But...."

"Oh you fool! Listen! I'll offer to pay for the rebuilding of any damaged property for free, people will trust me, then they will see that my boats are the best and rent them from me, so I will have succeeded in grabbing the whole of the fishing business in this village! The whole harbour will be mine."

Nasser understood his sophisticated plan but still not the "more serious" bit; that will come later, probably, he thought.

"So off you go with the others. Don't be confrontational. Be...be nice!" He struggled to find those last words in his mind and felt strange having uttered them.

"Yes sir. Straightaway." Nasser couldn't believe his ears, "nice"; he wanted to laugh but set out to accomplish the task immediately. As Nasser walked through the narrow corridor Abbas's words disturbed him more than usual. Abbas's reference to children in such a wicked mood made Nasser think that it was a sentiment that was secretly laced with jealousy. Years working under such a callous man made him suspect everything about him and when Nasser became a father Abbas's tone towards him was tinged with displeasure and annoyance. Abbas did not have children. Beyond the hatred, most knew that Abbas was a pitiable man, he did not experience love nor did he give it to others.

CHAPTER FOUR

Dangerous Help

A T long last the heavens relented and the rain ceased leaving the village drenched and flooded. Most of the villagers offered *Fajr prayer* on the rooftops of the sturdier buildings. After *Fajr* the village was silent. All that could be heard was the trickling of water; even the animals stood still and exhausted. The dusty streets of the village had turned to mud, branches and twigs were sticking out of rooftops, and soaked leaves and sprigs covered the lanes. The whitewashed walls were no longer white and a foul stench hung in the air: soon to be joined by mosquitoes and flies. School and work stalled for the day so everyone could assess the scale of the damage. Only farmers had to work today, otherwise their animals would go hungry. Even the fisherman slept in, their wooden boats were either flung far out to sea or were completely damaged. They wouldn't be fishing for a long time.

Intuitively the men went to the *masjid*. Ibrahim, Abdullah, Zaid, Hamza, Khalil and the Imam, all walking from different directions had found their way to the *masjid*. Though flooded and ruined, the *masjid* remained the centre of their communal life. They greeted each other with *assalamu'alaykum*. There was nowhere to sit as the floor was covered in puddles and the prayer mats were drenched so they stood in the main prayer hall with the *imam* standing beside the pulpit.

"*Al-Hamdulillah*, there does not seem to be any casualties," said the *imam*.

"Yes, that's the main thing. But my stocks of grain and rice are completely ruined," complained Hamza.

"Everyone has had some loss Hamza, Allah give us all patience." Ibrahim knew that Hamza's shop was almost destroyed, but he had to encourage him to be strong.

"Remember, Allah is with those who are patient," said Ibrahim.

"Of course Ibrahim, but we do need to think about some issues. The school roof, the minaret, the families from the hillsides, the damaged boats... and Ibrahim, your plans to leave," Abdullah spoke firmly. Khalil, Zaid and Hamza were relieved that Abdullah brought the subject up. "The village is in a real crisis. You cannot leave now," said Abdullah.

"Yes Ibrahim. We understand your predicament but the entire village has been affected and your presence is vital," the *imam* spoke earnestly. Ibrahim knew he would be hearing such words today so he didn't attempt to confront them.

"The village needs all of us, not just me, but don't worry I'll stay as long as I need to. *Insha' Allah*, we'll get things back to normal." His optimism and resolve made everyone smile, their hearts calmed by his words. "We all need to make extra *dua*," he added.

"Thank you so much Ibrahim," Khalil spoke quietly, holding back his tears. "Most of the boats are destroyed, my boats have gone. It's kind of people to keep us and help us but soon their own food and supplies will be exhausted and it will be unfair to burden them with our problems." Khalil turned away from the men and walked towards the window, where he took a deep breath and gazed out of the window.

"Ibrahim, Imam, my brothers," Zaid nodded at everyone while he spoke. "*Masha' Allah* everyone is being generous but there is only so much one can do. The school's roof needs to be fixed and work on some of the good homes can wait a little while but new homes need to be built immediately and these people need their livelihood too." Zaid, as always judged the situation well. "Even though it wasn't a typhoon it was nearly as bad. The damage can be seen for miles. The neighbouring villages have been badly hit too."

"Yes, Zaid, may Allah make things easy for everyone and protect us all from such calamities. Right then, for the next few hours let's tidy up the *masjid* and school. Later we'll meet to discuss matters further." Ibrahim wanted to get to work immediately as he did not have much time left in the village.

In Umer's home some cleaning and repairing was taking place; an attempt to recover from the storm. Zaynab mopped up the water on the veranda, while Umer, Ayesha and Fatima tidied the backyard.

"My father went to the hills early this morning. Most of the homes are wrecked," said Fatima, who was shocked by all the destruction but was delighted to be staying in Umer's nice home.

"Well, the village is in a mess. The minaret has been demolished and I overheard father say something about the school roof too," voiced Umer, a little glad with the thought of not having to go to school.

"But there was so much water, the rain kept coming – I didn't like it!" exclaimed Ayesha, as she picked twigs from the ground.

"Nobody liked it. Where's Hassan today?" asked Umer.

"Let's call for him." Fatima was tired of cleaning; *big houses need a lot of tidying up,* she thought to herself. Umer's house was only an average-sized home but she had never had the opportunity to sleep on a real bed under a real roof so to her this experience was something exceptional.

"Come on Ayesha, you can come too. Let's tell Ummi first." The three of them walked onto the back veranda, wiped their muddy feet on the rags laid there and went through the kitchen. The aroma of fried onions and garlic filled the kitchen but Aunty Ruqaiya had abandoned the stove and the pot of meat broth was boiling unattended. Suddenly his mother walked in.

"Hold on Ibrahim," she called out. She took a cloth in each hand, rolled it and held the pan by the handles and placed it on a nearby stand. Without acknowledging the children's presence she returned into the living room. The children knew what was happening – something too serious for them to be even noticed! They perched around the living room door.

Umer stretched his neck out a little more, as if to hear something.

"What is it?" asked Fatima, as usual, speaking too boldly at the wrong times.

"Ssh!" Umer and Ayesha chastised her with their expressions.

Their parents were talking. Umer knew he should not be eavesdropping but this time he couldn't help himself.

In the large room Zaynab was sorting through some old clothes. "Ruqaiya and Fatima need clothes, they don't have any." She made a pile of colourful garments for her friend and examined ones which needed to be altered so they would fit Fatima.

"Ibrahim, we must stay here to help out. It would not be right of us to abandon our friends." Zaynab was unaware of the children listening.

"Yes of course but I will not delay our leaving. The rest of the men will have to manage, they shouldn't keep depending on me."

"I suppose so, your new job is waiting too, and you have to honour that commitment."

"It was a bad storm and the village will have to see it through." Ibrahim was determined to go.

"The children will be unsettled but they'll manage. Poor Fatima, Ruqaiya doesn't know how to tell her that their home is totally destroyed. She will be devastated," Zaynab remarked with utter sadness, unaware that Fatima was close by.

Fatima suddenly felt so small, not like she usually felt when she admired others who had more than her. She felt she had no one, no home, nothing that she could call her own. Tears streamed down her face, her vision became blurred. No matter how shoddy it was, it was still her home. Wiping her face with her hands she turned and walked back out of the kitchen. Umer and Ayesha were speechless, neither could offer any words of consolation to her. Looking at each other they both realised that they should not have been eavesdropping. Umer, especially, felt ashamed and sad. "Allah please help her," he prayed.

❧ ❧

Zaid and Hamza made their way to Abdullah's house. Events had forced everyone to decide about what to do. A strange irony was being played out by the men of Tobay. Nearly all the men and women thought that Ibrahim and Abdullah were the only ones that could help the village out of this mess but strength was growing in the other men and their courage was unflinching.

"I can't believe it! He's still leaving!" exclaimed Zaid.

Abdullah met his guests on the veranda.

"Yes, we shouldn't be too surprised. We cannot expect him to stay. He has made other commitments." Abdullah understood Ibrahim's motives and was considering leaving himself.

"Come inside brothers so we can talk properly." Abdullah invited Zaid and Hamza into his home. The men walked through a spacious hallway into a room with padded armchairs. As one of the richest men in the village his home was large with decent furniture but it was not lavish or opulent. Abdullah was a wealthy but modest man – he never wasted his wealth on futile things.

The men sat down. "The new homes will be costly, the materials can be brought from the city. I will give as much as I can but the rest will have to come from others." Abdullah knew that the cost of everything - the new homes, the minaret, the school roof and new boats - was too much for him, despite his wealth.

Suddenly, with no eye contact from each other, the men thought of seeking help from Abbas. Perhaps they were hearing evil whispers. But they ignored it and in their own way, shuddered with the very idea of it. The whisperings vanished as their *imaan* was too strong. They discussed matters for about an hour, trying to find solutions to their problems.

Abdullah stood on the veranda and watched his friends leave. Maryam and her younger sister Hafsa watched from the balcony too, and their mother Halima, watched through a window on the first floor. Ironically, Abdullah and his family wanted to leave, but neither parent had the courage to voice their feelings. Halima was afraid for her daughter, living in a place where power is used to harm and destroy. Abdullah thought of discussing it with his wife but his pride got the better of him and he remained silent. *He did not want to be seen as running away.*

By early morning most of the puddles and pools had dried up but the ground was still damp and the smell lingered too. Most of the villagers were engaged in tidying up and a few of them prayed while they worked, asking for Allah's help and protection. Amidst them were a few men sent from the big house. They were clearly noticeable, especially with their neat and clean clothes. Hamza was sweeping outside his shop and around the back of his house. His wife, Jameela, had just caged their 'peculiar' cockerel. A young man approached Jameela.

"Aunty, do you need some help? Looks like you have a nasty bird there," he said.

She looked at him. Unease and fear made her breath faster. "No, I don't! Who are you?" She raised her voice because she didn't want to appear weak.

Hamza overheard. He dropped his broom and walked to the back of the house.

"Yes, who are you? What are you doing on my property?" He questioned him and looked at him carefully. *Those clothes are not from here, or the nearby villages and towns. Who is he?* Hamza knew these things, being a trader in almost everything.

"Well speak up boy!"

"Oh uncle, I was wondering if you need any help?" The man said smiling. Hamza understood. His blood began to boil. He could feel himself become red and hot. "Help? Your help! Are you out of your mind?" Hamza was a few yards away from the man. The young man started to look uneasy.

"Mr Hamza, you need help. You know you do. This shop is the lifeline of this village and......."

"Oh get off my property! *Lifeline of this village*! The fishing boats are the lifeline of this village and look at what your boss has done! Get out now! Before I beat you! We don't need your cheap help! I'll starve before I get help from Abbas!" Hamza roared so loudly that neighbours ran to witness the commotion.

"Alright! Alright! I'll go. But you need help, our help, so you better come to your senses quickly!" The man rushed out onto the lane and walked away quickly. Hamza followed him but then stopped. He was fuming like a volcano; his thoughts were like bubbling lava. Neighbours surrounded him and began to mutter while Jameela brandished the broom in one hand and the cockerel in the other.

Across the village at the school, Ibrahim was stacking stools and chairs in the yard. A few boys had been helping him earlier but they had returned home. He carried on patiently, not wanting to waste time. He heard footsteps. *Maybe someone has come to help.* Somehow he sensed something ominous. More footsteps could be heard. He left the chairs and walked around the school. "Yes, who is it? *Assalamu'alayk...*" He saw the men before he had the chance to finish. There was no reply to his greeting. It was Abbas, Nasser and another man.

"Well, well. The teacher is working hard." Abbas laughed, the sound of which was so vile that even the birds that had perched on the benches flew away.

"What is it?" Ibrahim went straight to the point. Abbas and Ibrahim glared into each other's eyes.

"No need to be so abrupt my dear fellow. We've come to see how you are doing. I can see that your school needs a lot of attention."

"Abbas, whatever your real intentions are, be aware that God is watching...."

"Oh please! Don't give me that God talk!"

"Of course, not. You've abandoned all faith, that's why you are the way you are." Ibrahim had waited a long time to speak to Abbas. In fact, they both had so many things to say to each other but never had the right opportunity.

Abbas smiled. He wanted to make Ibrahim so angry that he would burst out of his "righteousness," something he hated about Ibrahim. Ibrahim checked himself mentally.

At the gate of the school, Abbas's well-groomed horses attracted a handful of spectators, and the spectators attracted the attention of Abdullah and Zaid, who were on their way to the *masjid*.

"Shall we go to them?" asked Zaid.

"No, Ibrahim needs to say a few things to Abbas." Abdullah knew Ibrahim a little better than Zaid.

"I guess no harm will come to him. Everyone is there." Zaid observed the growing crowd.

Ibrahim continued with his work.

"We have quite an audience. These people think a lot of you Ibrahim... I don't know why but then they are just simple fisher folk."

Ibrahim walked over to Abbas, who was surprised at Ibrahim's response.

"Abbas, these people are not as simple as you think and you are not as great as you think. You are an oppressor. A bully who bullies poor people to get your pathetic way."

Anger became fury in Abbas and his servant felt embarrassed that his boss was spoken to like that.

"Be careful what you say, teacher! Otherwise I'll teach you a few lessons!"

"You? You Abbas, or your mercenaries? Look at you. You are a disgrace! You couldn't even come to see me without your bodyguards. That's how small and weak you are!"

Nasser felt strange. He realised that he shouldn't be there with Abbas. The other man edged closer to Ibrahim. Nasser held him back. "No! It's not our fight," he said to the other servant. Strangely to him, Nasser found himself praying silently, '*Astagfirullah, astagfirullah.*'

Zaid and Abdullah could no longer watch from amidst the crowd. Dozens of villagers ran to see the confrontation between the men. Shy-veiled women looked directly at the man they so loathed and meek farmers pushed others to get closer to the man whom everyone was afraid to confront.

"Get those horses off school property now!" Zaid instructed the man standing beside Nasser. The man complied, totally baffled at being made to feel scared.

"Abbas! You really are half a man, with no respect or dignity! How dare you come here and speak to Ibrahim like that!" Abdullah was stern. He felt guilty for even thinking of seeking Abbas's help.

"If you have something to say, say it and be on your way," said Abdullah.

"Abdullah, you sound just like these common people, but I will be on my way. I came here to offer my help. My financial help, for the rebuilding of this school and that place of worship." Abbas turned to the crowd. "And to anyone else who needs money to rebuild their homes. Just come to see Nasser and he will make the arrangements for you. I am not a bad man, as these men make me out to be. They don't like me. After all, if I was so bad why would I want to help you all?" Abbas was at the peak of his treacherous plot. He glanced over the heads of the gathered crowd. Unfortunately most of the simple villagers believed in his words and began to smile at him. "So come and see us." Abbas was pleased with himself; he felt his influence increasing. It would only be a matter of time before the village and it's people were his, he thought.

"Wait a minute! What about the harbour? Your men have been burning the boats so the fishermen can't use them." Zaid spoke as loud as he could, so everyone could hear him.

"No proof! No evidence! No proof!" Abbas waved his pointed finger about. "Oh Ibrahim, you should not leave the village in such a state. Don't run away from your duty." Abbas was playing with the weaknesses of the village like soft clay in his hands.

"You are a liar and a tyrant! Get off the school grounds now!" Ibrahim ordered.

"Yes, well the offer still stands. Don't let your own ego get into the way of the children's education."

"Since when have you been concerned for our children? You don't even have any! You are a lonely little man!" Abdullah meant every word he said and his words hurt Abbas the most. Like a knife driven deep into his heart.

Cruelty was never an aspect of Abdullah's character but he couldn't help himself. Nearly every man in Tobay was a father and a husband and the constant threat to their families was too much to bear. Abdullah knew he had said what would hurt Abbas the most.

"Let's go!" Abbas could not make eye contact with anyone. The unwelcomed men mounted their horses and rode away.

"People!" Ibrahim appealed to the crowd. "We don't need his help, only Allah's help. Just ignore him..... he is a dangerous man. Please!" Ibrahim pleaded. The expressions of most of the villagers betrayed them. It was too late. The promise of help, especially financial help, was irresistible to them in these desperate times. Most of these people were from the hills and their homes were totally destroyed. Suddenly the fear they had of the man responsible for so many crimes vanished and instead they looked towards Abbas as the only source of help.

CHAPTER FIVE

The Letter

L USTROUS shades of crimson, blue and purple, with ripples of dusky orange covered the dawn sky. The early morning dew glazed the thick foliage of the trees. Birds flew effortlessly and peacefully at this tranquil time of the day. Men wearing white left the *masjid* as *Fajr* prayer was over. The village began to stir, and some farmers were already out in the fields starting their daily toil. Some homes were filled with the smell of freshly brewed tea and homemade bread, and lanterns were still lit, as the true light of the day had not yet emerged.

In Umer's home the children were sitting around a small wooden table in the kitchen. Despite the delicious breakfast of eggs, bread, milk and biscuits, Fatima found it almost impossible to gulp anything down. Her shattered home was on her mind and the other children knew this.

"Please Fatima, have some biscuits. There's sugar too for the milk." Ayesha pushed a platter of biscuits towards Fatima. There was no response. She felt like an outsider, so insignificant and alone. There was a knock at the door. "I'll go and see. Cheer up Fatima," Umer dashed out of the kitchen.

Zaynab opened the front door. It was Maryam and Hafsa. "*Assalamu'alaykum* girls. It's very early for you two to be out," she enquired.

"*Wa'alaykum as-salam*. My mother knows we have come here. We thought Fatima might need some cheering up. We heard she never ate anything last night, so we've brought her some yoghurt and bread," explained Maryam, with little Hafsa by her side.

Umer joined them. "*Assalamu'alaykum*. Thank you for the parcel of food. She needs it. Mother can they join us?" Umer asked his mother.

"Yes, of course. Go straight through girls."

It was sometime before Fatima ate something and after breakfast the children decided to play in the yard. Ibrahim set out for another day of cleaning the school. He saw the children in the yard.

"Children, I expect you all to be in school in half an hour to tidy up. Especially you Umer. You should know your duties. But go on, you can play for a while." Although Ibrahim needed the help, he didn't like to disturb the children's games; the children needed to be engrossed in their innocent games to stay aloof from the bigger, more dangerous reality that the adult world was embroiled in.

The schoolyard was noisy. Stacks of chairs and stools kept collapsing and a dozen brooms were being bashed against the ground in an effort to make their school really clean, and as usual the children giggled and chatted. Safiya, Zaid's daughter, joined Maryam, Ayesha, Fatima and Hafsa. It was the first time this week that she left her home because of her father's over-protectiveness.

Ibrahim took a ladder and was doing something to the roof or what was left of it and the boys attempted to stack the tables neatly.

"Nice to see you Bilal. Did you go on holiday?" Hassan remarked. "Or maybe you went to jail! Well, where were you?"

"Give him a chance Hassan. Where have you been?" Umer had a more polite tone.

"My father was worried about things in the village so he kept us home." Bilal was a quiet and shy boy and he enjoyed staying at home.

"Well, lots of work here so give a helping hand," said Hassan. Hassan and Bilal moved some tables.

"Things are changing you know Hassan. People are changing, my father says we should always strive to be good and honest, and stay away from the trouble-makers." Umer was trying to summarise the village news.

"Umer, I saw a few families walk across the fields over to the big house. Is that bad?" Bilal sensed it was but couldn't quite articulate it to himself.

"Probably getting help from Mr Rich," said Hassan, who carried on working without becoming emotionally involved.

"Well, I think it is bad. I wouldn't get help from such a person." Umer had learnt a lot about Abbas and his scheming. "We should stay away from bad people."

"Yeah, stick with us Bilal. I'll look after you. I've got the strength and Umer has the big talk."

"Hassan, Allah is the Protector. Don't joke about serious stuff." Umer was a little annoyed at Hassan's attitude. Hassan quickly changed the subject.

"Anyway, Abrar, goes to the *masjid* now. Do you know that Bilal?"

"Really? Things are changing!" Bilal was shocked.

"Abrar's alright, we should welcome him not talk behind his back." Umer was quick to defend Abrar.

"But his father helps, you know *him*." Bilal was even frightened to say the name.

"You mean Abbas. Can't people be strong, like the books teach us!" Umer left his stacking and went over to Hassan and Bilal. "Look, his father has been seen at the *masjid* too. So maybe he is changing."

"But who does all the bad stuff then?" Hassan probed.

"We all know it's Abbas's men but we don't know the actual individuals who have done it. Anyway, even if he did do some bad things, he is changing for the better. Maybe he has asked Allah to forgive him. And if Allah can forgive, then what's your problem Hassan?"

"My problem, no problem at all. I'm just cleaning the school like a good person. No problem!" Hassan sensed Umer's tone – he did not want to argue with him, especially when Umer was right.

Imam Abdurrahman appeared from behind the fence, "*Assalamu'alaykum* boys."

"*Wa'alaykum as-salam* Imam," they chorused.

The *imam* saw Ibrahim on the ladder. "Carry on up there, just checking on the boys. And good to hear some good words from you Umer *Masha' Allah*. Keep it up!"

"Thank you Imam." Umer was pleased and reassured.

"I expect you boys to be at the *masjid* to tidy up later." Then the Imam turned and began walking across the yard. "*Assalamu'alaykum* boys, and nice to see you Bilal." The children resumed their jobs.

Another breakfast was being served far away, an extravagant breakfast in Abbas's house. He sat at the end of a large oval table, with a dozen or so dishes and an elaborate teapot in front of him. This morning the breakfast did not look so appetising and Abbas looked different too. His face was weary and his eyes puffy. Somehow his strength and arrogance had diminished. In his mind, yesterday's events swirled around and most of all Abdullah's words, a scorpion sting to his ego, but not to his conscience. Nasser opened the door and walked in. No greeting or eye contact came from him.

Abbas was always sharp enough to notice changes in his workers but today he did not reprimand Nasser. Instead he thought of Nasser having children of his own, while he worked for him. Yet, with all his wealth, he still had no son of his own to share it with. He had been married for only a short time and was quite happy. Then tragedy struck him and his wife died from a serious illness. His grieving was veiled by his greed and treachery but he missed his wife and knew very well that his wealth could not bring her back. Abbas did not attempt to remarry. He clutched on to the only way of living he knew which revolved around making more wealth. He had gained so much with his wealth but he could not attain a wife and a family through which sometimes he would escape from his own vices. This discreet longing for a companion was deeply embedded in some crevice of his mind but rejection and his own persona made it rotten and contemptible.

Nasser placed some papers beside Abbas and turned to leave.

"Nasser, send Tariq in. I have some matters to discuss with him."

"Yes sir." Nasser left without questioning what the "matters" were, for he didn't care. Nasser walked through hallways and down sets of stairs, through a large hall and out of the house. *It's time I left this place. I need to take my family elsewhere,* he thought. He headed towards his home, which was on Abbas's estate, behind the hill, totally hidden from the viewpoint of the village.

Regret, remorse and sadness swelled inside him. He felt his wrong actions were too great to walk away from, perhaps even too great for forgiveness. For had he not personally set fire to dozens of boats just before the fishing season? Had he not set fire to the ripe rice crop just before the harvest so that the farmers in their desperation would be forced to sell their land to Abbas? Had he not poisoned the watering well where a particularly stubborn farmer unwilling to sell his land, gave water to his animals? These animals became sick and some even died. He had done all this and more but he could not carry on like this. His sincere remorse at his actions invited a strange sense of faith, hope, fear and seeking of forgiveness all rolled into one. He knew what he should do. First, he planned to go to the *masjid*, and spend some time there. The *masjid* always gave him something, a sense of peace and comfort that filled all the holes of his heart made by his conscience-pricking activities. *I'm going to change. I won't be a slave to him anymore. I need to find my faith and use it,* he thought to himself. Then he headed into the village.

Zaynab was busy folding blankets and sheets and Ruqaiya helped her put them neatly into a large basket. The veranda was filled with boxes of books, bags of clothes and baskets of household items. Preparation was underway for leaving, they had just a week left. Zaynab felt a little tearful packing her things away, as this was her second home after she married Ibrahim. So many memories were set in the walls and furniture here. But life is a journey, she said to herself, believers shouldn't be attached to one place, sometimes we have to move for the better.

Another part of Zaynab felt that they were fleeing from the situation and the strength that once emanated from those who were seen as strong was diminishing. She felt that this could only be replenished by her husband standing up to confront Abbas's violent design for the village and its people. Zaynab knew that Ibrahim was the total opposite of Abbas. Ibrahim was generous and kind whereas Abbas was selfish and mean. She also knew that Abbas was more powerful than her husband but she was not afraid of Abbas. Everyone held Zaynab in high regard as she spoke courteously and gave everyone their due respect, and like the people of the village, she was burdened by Abbas's insatiable desire to own everything and everyone around him.

Ruqaiya sensed Zaynab's thoughts, "Don't worry, *Insha' Allah* you will be fine." Zaynab smiled, but felt embarrassed as she had the security of moving into a proper home and Ruqaiya's family still had no idea what they would do about settling into a home.

Ibrahim returned home. "*Assalamu'alaykum*. How is the packing going? I'll help you today *Insha' Allah*."

"*Wa'alaykum as-salam*. I'll manage, you just deal with the school. I've got Ruqaiya and the children here." Zaynab was considerate of her husband's duty to the school.

Abdullah appeared at the front steps of the house. "*Assalamu'alaykum*. Can I come in?"

"*Wa'alaykum as-salam*. Yes, come through. We'll sit inside." Ibrahim led the way into the lounge. "Please sit down."

Abdullah did not make himself comfortable in his chair. Sleepless nights and the current situation in Tobay had forced Abdullah to make a decision. How would Ibrahim take his news? He guessed he would take it well but what about the others? Abdullah had helped many people in the past but these new challenges were different.

"Ibrahim, my wife and I have been discussing some issues. She is very afraid, especially for our daughters. She says that without the support of this family in the village, especially Umer's mother, it will be difficult."

"What are you trying to say my brother?"

"We hope to leave the village too." Abdullah expected to hear some negative words but after all it was Ibrahim he was talking too.

"*Al-Hamdulillah*. I had a feeling you would consider it. You have your own land and good financial support, so it will be easy for you, *Insha' Allah*."

"Yes, but wealth is not everything." Abdullah valued the village people highly and this had made his decision to leave very difficult. "People who are sincere and good make living in a place easy. We have been brought up in this village. We go back a long way."

"Yes but life has changed since these problems came about, despite the good people like Zaid, Hamza, Khalil and the imam."

"Perhaps they can come as well. It's too much stress living in a place where there is a tyrant who abuses people right before our eyes and you can't do anything about it. I'm not running away, I'm afraid for my family." Abdullah was honest, and felt relief after sharing his load.

"I really do think the others could manage leaving, if they really wanted to. We will be moving into the home of the teacher who is coming here, a swap of jobs and homes. Accommodation should be easy to find there, it is a bigger place than Tobay, it's a big town." Ibrahim hoped his other friends would join him.

"I'll keep my property here, maybe rent it out, and I'll buy something new there. Allah make it easy for us all." Abdullah prayed silently for everyone.

"*Ameen*. Abdullah have some tea with me then come to the harbour. We should check how things are there. Maybe we can help them a little."

"Of course. We need to see Khalil, and give him our moral support. It was brave of him to reject Abbas's handouts but some of the others have taken it. Despite what has happened".

"Abdullah, situations like this illustrate that faith is an invaluable gift that helps us through the difficult times, like poverty. For people who have little or no faith hardship is like a disease that eats away their senses. Only the ones with firm faith can deal with poverty with dignity. Khalil is one of them. Anyway, let's drink tea then we can go." The men had a light breakfast then headed to the harbour.

Anger was fermenting in the big house. Abbas stomped up and down his very large lounge waiting for Tariq and Nasser. The heavy breakfast he had consumed made his stomach full and his chest tight. He took out a white

handkerchief from his waistcoat pocket and wiped the
sweat from his bald head and face. He looked at the
embroidered initials on the corner of the handkerchief.
It was his father's. A strange sensation overcame him. He
gazed at it carefully but refused to be moved by the memory
of his loving father and the sentiments it unearthed. He
screwed the handkerchief into a small ball and flicked it on
the floor not looking to see where it landed. This incident
augmented what was really bothering him; his impatience
could not mask what really disturbed him and in addition
this aggravation caused indigestion. If only he could have
prevented Abdullah from saying what he had: Abdullah who
was strong and handsome, with a caring wife and beautiful
children. He needed to expel his rage and frustration. He
would shout at his men, he thought to himself.

"Where is that Nasser? I should have known he's
changing! *Thinking* too much!" He slammed the door and
left the room. He searched for him in the rooms where Nasser
usually worked, doing Abbas's paperwork and accounting.
He found him in one room sitting on the floor on a prayer
mat. Nasser was holding his face and murmuring. Abbas
did not know what to do. He walked slowly towards him.
Rage overwhelmed him. He carefully lifted a vase from a
nearby table and smashed it on Nasser's head. Nasser fell
down in shock and fear overtook him. Blood ran down his
forehead and a dull pain throbbed in his head.

"*Astagfirullah, astagfirullah*," Nasser prayed for forgiveness
as he thought about punishment and death. Then he saw
Abbas and realised what had happened to him.

"You disgusting little traitor. Get up and get to work."
Without any thought or remorse Abbas left the room.

Tariq was in the hallway. "You, Tariq, come to my room. I've had enough of this lot. It's time I taught them a lesson they'll never forget!" All the old strength, arrogance and vigour had awoken in Abbas, he was back to his normal self.

Nasser held his head. Wetness seeped through his fingers. Gingerly he brought his crimson hands in front of his eyes, so close that his tears mingled with the blood that had pooled in the creases of his palms. With the back of his hand he wiped his eyes and dusted bits of porcelain from his clothes. His head hurt, it hurt more now than the actual blow. As he stood up he was almost overwhelmed by dizziness and dark clouds drifted before his eyes and blurred his vision. Nasser held on to the back of a nearby chair to gather his thoughts and replenish his courage that his boss would have liked to destroy completely. He straightened his back and gritted his teeth. His reflection from a large mirror opposite him caught him unaware. Nasser looked at his broad shoulders and thick neck. *Where is my strength?* he asked himself. He knew for certain it was not with Abbas nor was it with him while he was in that monstrous house.

⚜ ⚜

The sun was at its zenith and the air was still and motionless. At the beach, the ocean's streaks of aquamarine and blue merged into the distant sky. The glistening sand was soft and clean, and small waves splashed on the shore. Abdullah and Ibrahim walked along the beach; the golden sand sank beneath their feet and the clean air carried traces of salt from the ocean. They walked for three miles before reaching the harbour. Khalil was busy at work.

"*Assalamu'alaykum*, Ibrahim and Abdullah. What are you two doing here?" Khalil was pleased to see them.

"*Wa'alaykum as-salam*. We just thought we'd better check how things are here. Are you mending your boats?" asked Ibrahim.

"Yes, with whatever tools I have, I'm getting some materials from Hamza."

"You are wise not to fall into Abbas's trap," remarked Abdullah.

"It doesn't take wisdom to work out what Abbas really wants. He's buying people's hearts and minds, and pretty soon he'll have their land and homes too. Not me. I'll make do with little rather than fall into his trap. Khalil stepped out of his boat, bent down and brushed clean two planks of wood.

"Please sit down." Khalil pointed to the planks.

"*Jazak Allah*, we'll sit but not for long. There's lots of work to do at the school, and I have to pack my books too," said Ibrahim, a gentle way of letting Khalil know he was leaving.

"So you're still going? We thought you would stay, or at least stay a few months." Khalil felt dejected.

"The village will cope. I made my mind to go before the storm and I'm leaving in a few days." Ibrahim did not make eye contact with Khalil. He felt a little ashamed that his words were hurtful to his friend.

"I understand. Everyone has their own burden to carry. Allah will help us." Khalil realised he should be stronger.

"We'd better go now Ibrahim." Abdullah didn't want to upset Khalil either.

"Yes." Both men stood up. "Khalil I'm honoured that you are my brother. You've stood up to Abbas even when those around you have faltered." Ibrahim wanted Khalil to feel positive about himself and his situation.

"I know it's hard for those who have lost almost everything, but the people who have accepted Abbas's financial help need to realise that in a few days he'll be forcing those same people to use his boats. Then he will finally have monopoly over them," said Abdullah.

"I don't know why he wants control over the village," said Khalil.

"Because some men crave power and glory. But only Allah is glorious and has power over all things. Abbas has no faith and morals." Ibrahim summed up Abbas's character.

"Anyway, glad to see you are strong and not letting events divert you. Take care. *Assalamu'alaykum*," said Ibrahim.

"*Assalamu'alaykum*," said Abdullah.

"*Wa'alaykum as-salam* and thank you for coming." Khalil appreciated his friends concern. The men shook hands. Ibrahim and Abdullah walked away reflecting on Khalil's situation.

"Brother Ibrahim how about taking a walk around the outskirts of the village, like the good old days?" Abdullah reminisced.

"Yes, why not? We used to walk a lot when we were school children, many years ago."

"You mean many decades ago!" laughed Abdullah. On such a jolly note the men set off.

❧ ❧

The *masjid* was getting busy now. It was much cleaner and organised too. Imam Abdurrahman was carefully fitting light bulbs into their sockets and others were sweeping outside. Half of the prayer hall was covered with rows of brown and red prayer mats.

In the corner sat a man. He was praying for forgiveness and guidance. His thoughts about his past made him shake his head with remorse. There were tears in his eyes and sincerity in his heart. The man had a large wound on his forehead, with dry matted blood. It was Nasser.

Zaid removed his shoes and entered the *masjid*. Carrying rolls of prayer mats that had been washed and dried, he walked into the main prayer hall. Nasser caught his attention immediately. Unlike his usual self, Zaid reacted patiently and he realised that being more patient offered him more time to think about what to say and do. He placed the rolls of mats to one side and walked over to Nasser. As he drew closer Nasser's wound became visible. He sat next to him.

"Nasser?"

Nasser looked at him. What a difference the wound had made to Nasser and to Zaid. In Zaid's eyes Nasser appeared like a good but tormented man, no longer tormenting, and to Nasser, Zaid's facial expression was welcoming, no longer condemning.

"I'm sorry, for everything."

"Nasser, I gather you no longer work for Abbas?"

Nasser nodded.

"He did that to you, didn't he?"

Nasser nodded again.

"Don't worry, we'll help you. What is it?" Zaid was courageous and supportive.

"My wife and son are there. We have a small home on his estate. I don't know how to get them out."

"Come on. No time to waste. I'll see how Abbas tries to harm you now. Let's go."

Both men left the *masjid*. They did not know that the *imam* had unintentionally overheard their conversation, as he climbed the *minbar* to fix the lamp there. And what the *imam*, Zaid, and Nasser did not know, was that Umer and Hassan had overheard the conversation intentionally. As the boys arrived to help out they peeped through the arched window just behind where Nasser was sitting and heard everything.

"Shall we go Umer?" Hassan was excited. To him most things were a game.

"No. It's dangerous. We could get in the way. They need to get Abrar and his mum out safely." Umer was being responsible and cautious.

"But we could go just to have a look."

"No. Not everything is a game." Umer frowned at his naïve friend. "I hope Abrar will be alright. *Insha' Allah*."

"Boys! Boys! Stop chatting and get inside, straight to work," called the *imam*. The boys went inside the *masjid* and began unrolling and arranging the clean prayer mats.

Zaid walked close to Nasser as they made their way through the village. He did this to show onlookers that they were friends not foes. Occasionally Zaid would put his arm around Nasser, as if to stop him from falling, but Nasser knew well that Zaid would never let him fall now that he had taken him as a friend. Nasser could not believe the generosity Zaid was showing. He admired his determination and unwavering strength against a man whom he himself had been physically fearful of, even though Nasser towered over his boss in height. Nasser felt strengthened by Zaid's resolve and his willingness to help. As both men walked, their thoughts and emotions were brewing into a determination that two other men, who were close friends, had yet to muster.

It was turning out to be a pleasant day for the girls. Despite their disappointment at not being chosen to help out at the *masjid* they enjoyed being at school together. Now that their job was done they made their way home. Safiya had already left earlier with her brother Bilal.

"I'm glad you're much happier now Fatima," said Maryam.

"Yes, I love our school. I'll do anything for it." Fatima was proud of her school.

"Shall we take a longer route home today?" Ayesha was unsurprisingly daring, but none of the girls noticed.

"Yes, alright then, but we shouldn't take too long." Maryam said with little real fear. This afternoon the girls were different, they were daring and complacent. It was as if every little piece of advice their mothers had given them over the years, about safety and obedience, had been forgotten by them.

"Ayesha, don't you think Hassan is too cheeky? He makes me angry," said Fatima.

"Yes, definitely. But he's my brother's best friend. He's scared of Umer. Umer is strong, you see." Ayesha admired her brother, despite their occasional sibling arguments.

"We don't have any brothers," remarked Hafsa, innocently.

"I will miss playing with you when you leave." Maryam did not know about her family's plan to move.

"I will too, especially seeing Umer beat Hassan!" laughed Fatima.

"Yes, I'll miss our games but my mother says we are growing up now. And soon we won't be able to play together." Ayesha suddenly remembered her mother telling her and Umer: *"there comes a time when boys and girls stop playing games together. You are all ten, eleven or twelve. Umer is thirteen, but in a year or so you girls will not be able to play out with the boys. It is not the Muslim way. You will be growing into young Muslim ladies..."*

"My mum says the same. I still don't understand why," said Maryam.

"Never mind all that. Why don't we plan a final game? Because Ayesha and Umer are leaving. A really good game." Fatima was excited and bright-eyed.

"Yes, yes. We should," Hafsa cried out.

"Shall we? I mean we could if we wanted to." Maryam was thrilled with the idea.

"Yes, we'll plan it our way. I have an idea. Let's go to my house first." Ayesha assumed the role of the leader and led the girls as they ran down the lane towards her home.

Zaynab and Ruqaiya were preparing the evening meal. Ruqaiya sat cross-legged in the kitchen on a small wooden stool, no higher than half a foot. In front of her was a small wooden table with a large fish. She clasped the fish under its gills with one hand and with the other hand held a sharp knife with which she scraped off its scales. The silvery scales dispersed into the air, and fell on the floor and on her clothes. Zaynab sat nearby chopping okra and aubergines. On the stove behind them a pan of boiling rice filled the kitchen with a starchy aroma. They heard the playful talk of the girls as they entered the garden.

Once inside, the girls went into Ayesha's bedroom. They sat down on her neatly made bed. Hafsa's hair was unusually messy. Maryam made her sit on the bed and began undoing her plaits. Her hair glistened from the almond oil her mother would put on it. Maryam took the comb that lay on a nearby cabinet and began combing her sister's hair in a motherly fashion. Hafsa sat quietly but smiled at Fatima who watched the two sisters with a little envy.

Ayesha rummaged around in a drawer with concentration.

"Found them," she said, pushing the drawer shut with her hip as she faced the others. "Candy sticks! I got this a long time ago and I hid it from Umer then I forgot about it!" Ayesha held a long piece of candy. She bit off a piece and gave it to Fatima who put it into her mouth with no hesitation or thanks. Ayesha bit off pieces for Maryam and Hafsa who inspected the dusty lumps before they placed them in their mouths.

"I'll get some paper," said Ayesha.

"What for?" questioned Fatima.

"To write a mystery letter! Umer started that game of mystery letters. We can write one too!" Maryam burst out; she had never been so excited.

"Yes, now listen," ordered Ayesha. "Since nobody says bad things about the harbour anymore. We'll play hide and seek there, because it has all the best hiding places."

"Sounds really good. What do we need the paper for?" asked Fatima.

"We'll leave a letter for Umer. By the time he reads it we'll be hiding in the boats. Umer and Hassan have to find all of us before *Maghrib* and get us back to our homes before dark otherwise they'll be in deep trouble." Ayesha was delighted with her master plan.

"We could get in trouble!" Maryam said.

"No, you know they will get us out before dark. They're good at this game," said Fatima.

"I don't know. I'm a little scared but I want to go and have fun," said Maryam.

"Yes, come on. Maryam, it will be fun," Hafsa exclaimed.

"Now let me write. Be quiet." Ayesha began to write. She read aloud as she wrote:-

To Umer and Hassan

We have decided to plan a final game because Umer is leaving. We are hidden far away in treasure boxes, near a deep blue sea, captured by pirates. Come and save us before dark otherwise there will be lots of trouble for you both!

From Ayesha, Fatima, Maryam and Hafsa.

"Does it sound good?" asked Ayesha.

"Brilliant. They'll run to get us!" Fatima jumped up and down. Hafsa joined her.

"How much time do we have?" Maryam asked.

"It's nearly *Asr* time. We should make our way there now." Ayesha ordered.

The girls smuggled themselves out of the house and were on their way to the beach. With excitement bubbling inside them the girls ran ahead. Not one of them remembered anything good taught by their parents. They had already forgot to pray their *Zuhr* and now they were about to miss their *Asr salah* too. Their childish games overtook them completely. While their mothers were talking about homes and furniture, and while their fathers were dealing with work matters, their daughters, and at the same time, their sons too, were being exposed to a dangerous sea of games due to their excitement and immaturity. Knowledge of all things belongs to Allah, and only after time would the families know if the children had survived the tidal waves, or drowned in the deep ocean for eternity.

CHAPTER SIX

Chasing Fear

ATTITUDES were not so different in Abbas's home too. With Nasser's apparent betrayal on his mind, Abbas frantically paced around his room. His servant, Tariq, waited patiently. Eventually Abbas stopped. He wiped the sweat from his forehead and sat down on his chair. Abbas's face lit up and became gleeful, he had thought of what to do.

"Yes, sir?" Tariq tried to draw some words out of him.

"Yes, Tariq. You see, the situation at the moment could get worse. These people's minds have been clouded by one individual, that petty little teacher. And as he is still going to leave, others might follow him. Although we haven't heard anything yet."

"Well actually, sir," Tariq interrupted, daringly. "One of my juniors has found out that maybe...I say maybe, Abdullah may also be leaving."

Abbas clenched his fist and swung it in the air. "You see! You see! Others will follow too." Who will work the harbour if many more leave? He thought to himself.

"Listen carefully. Take some men..."

In the hallway a boy was listening and watching through the keyhole. It was Abrar, Nasser's son. He had come to find his father. Abrar wasn't allowed in the house but since Abbas hardly left his lounge or bedroom, the workers allowed him in. For some, a fresh innocent face in the house, gave them hope that things could get better, even for them, working as they did in this dark house. Abrar overheard the conversation. He couldn't believe what he heard. His heart pounded harder and louder.

"Don't wait for the night to do it. Get to work straight away. Let the whole village see it. They'll be shocked out of their senses. That will teach them!" Criminal fury defined Abbas's present mindset, his words were heinous .

Abrar moved away from the door and ran down the hallway. He rushed out of the house to tell his mother. *If only my father was here...*

"I can't believe it!" shouted Hamza. Zaid grabbed his arm pulling him out of the shop.

"We must go now!"

Nasser was waiting outside, shame and guilt marked his appearance.

"Don't say anything to Nasser, he's been through enough." Zaid was already defending Nasser. Hamza took one look at Nasser and realised what had happened.

"Don't worry, we'll help you," nodded Hamza.

The men began to run down the lane, leaving Hamza's wife totally baffled as she watched the three men disappear into the distance.

The men reached Abbas's grand garden, puffing and panting.

"Come this way. I know a back entrance into the compound. If we go directly they will see us." Nasser led the way, behind the walled garden, which was overgrown with weeds and thorns. "I wish I went home first," cried out Nasser. "I should have protected my family first. But I felt compelled to go the *masjid*."

"Stop torturing yourself. We'll get your family out," Zaid reassured him.

Nasser led them behind the stables and old barn. Zaid and Hamza could not believe their eyes. It was as if they were in another village or town. Ahead of them were stables, little stone homes for the workers, and further on gardens with ceramic fountains. Nasser noticed the men's gaze.

"Please hurry, don't be too overwhelmed with all these riches. Each house and horse has been bought with the sweat of those poor people. May Allah forgive me for my sins!" Nasser spoke with disgust as his deeds of the past few years churned up in his mind. Hamza and Zaid knew exactly what he meant. These riches were false and unjustly acquired, through the oppression of the weaker people.

"Yes, yes. Which way now?" Hamza asked.

"Over there, near the tall fountain." Nasser pointed to his home. With great care, and *duas*, the men walked over to the house. Nasser entered first. Hamza and Zaid waited nervously, trying to hide themselves behind the bushes. They could hear voices.

"What! My God! He's gone too far! Never! I'll stop him myself! Never! Get your things quickly! Now!" Nasser screamed from inside. Zaid and Hamza frowned at each other through the branches and leaves. Nasser stuck his head out of the door.

"Listen," he whispered. "My son has overheard Abbas planning something crazy! We need to go urgently! I'll explain on the way."

Abrar and his mother came out of the house. The men took the bags and bundles from them and they all left carefully. By the grace of Allah, no one saw them enter and no one saw them leave.

꩜

Tranquillity filled the room where Zaynab and Ruqaiya sat quietly making *dhikr*, as they mended a torn patchwork quilt. Sitting at the opposite ends of the quilt, they stitched ripped squares of pink and green cotton onto a white quilt. Suddenly Maryam's mother barged in, without a knock or greeting. She had been crying. Zaynab immediately sensed trouble.

"What is it?" Zaynab asked.

"The girls are not at home. They have left without my permission. I don't know where they are." She began to weep. Zaynab and Ruqaiya put their needles and fabric down.

"Sister, don't worry," Zaynab said falsely as she began to worry too. "We heard them come in earlier." Zaynab called out for them. She called out again but louder. There was no response. Zaynab's head spun with confusion.

"You know that my girls never, never, leave without my permission." Maryam's mother began to sob, instead of thinking about where her daughter could be.

"Calm down. Let me check their room." Zaynab led the way. "Maybe they're having an afternoon nap," she said unrealistically. The room was empty. A strange feeling of fear and horror grew inside them.

"Look!" Ruqaiya pointed at the letter left on Umer's bed. Zaynab picked the letter up and read it in a few seconds. Dread covered her face.

"Oh Allah! Please help those girls! Those stupid children!"

Maryam's mother took the letter and read aloud as Ruqaiya could not read. Ruqaiya stood close to Maryam and peered at the written letters with curiosity.

"Oh no! They could be in danger!" shouted Ruqaiya.

"Let's calm down. First we need to get there but their fathers need to know too."

Zaynab was finding it hard to think clearly. If the women went without notifying anyone, especially their husbands, and came across trouble then who would help them? Most men had told their wives to stay away from the harbour too, especially since Abbas's helpers would frequently roam around the place looking for trouble.

"Shall we just go? If we see someone on the way we'll tell them." Ruqaiya was worried about Fatima; she knew very well what mischief she could get up to.

"Yes, come on. I don't think any real danger will come to them. Things have calmed down at the harbour now." Zaynab tried to pacify everyone including herself. She had not burst out like that for years and was now feeling a little embarrassed. Zaynab and Ruqaiya put on their *hijaabs* and they all left. All the while Maryam's mother cried and Ruqaiya had her arm around her, while Zaynab prayed every single prayer she could think of. She really wanted Allah's help. As they stepped out of the house Zaynab could see that Halima was not about to stop her crying.

Her whimpering began to annoy Zaynab a little, as it was vital that they all remained alert and calm.

The sky showed signs of *Maghrib* time as it lost some of its brightness. Farmers with fat-tailed sheep rounded their small herds and took short cuts across the village by taking the lanes instead of sticking to the fields. Slow huge buffalo moved sluggishly ahead of men sitting on carts. The carts carried a variety of Tobay's finest harvest: balls of citrus fruit could be seen between the gaps in the boxes, small limes, oval-shaped lemons and tangerines and satsumas of different hues of orange. Deep purple aubergines made a contrast with baskets of green beans and bunches of leafy spinach with pink roots. The women were being slowed down by this traffic, they were trapped behind the buffalo and a young man with his handful of black and white goats. After ten minutes the farmers dispersed allowing the women space to move freely.

The women walked past the *masjid*. Voices called from behind the fence of the *masjid*.

"Mother! Aunty! Ummi!"

The women turned. They looked at the *masjid*. From the outside, the *masjid* still looked badly beaten from the typhoon and the missing minaret added to its strange appearance. A few men were sweeping outside the *masjid* and the women's startled demeanour caught their attention. They could see they were distressed but did not venture into asking them. Umer and Hassan raced towards them. As usual Hassan was faster than Umer. They halted in front of the women. Zaynab did not greet them with a smile and Halima's tears made the boys more uneasy. Immediately Umer knew his mother was disturbed.

"What's wrong Ummi?" he asked.

"Your sister and the others have gone to the harbour," Zaynab snapped.

The men sweeping outside the *masjid* could not help but overhear. Visions of men stabbing others and all sorts of brutality filled Halima's head.

Ruqaiya noticed the men staring at them. The men abandoned their cleaning and began whispering amongst themselves. She noticed that they were fishermen whom her husband often went out to sea with.

"To the harbour?" questioned Umer.

"Yes!" She replied.

"When?" Hassan asked.

"Read this!" Zaynab thrust the letter towards Umer.

"Oh no! Ummi, Ummi!" Umer was afraid and angry. So was Hassan.

"Tell them Umer. Tell them now." Hassan realised things were getting out of hand.

"What is it? Tell us," said Ruqaiya.

The boys were quiet. "Now!" shouted Maryam's mum, who came out of her sobbing shell.

"Ummi, I think things are getting bad. You see, we heard...... We also found out that Abrar's father, Mr Nasser was beaten up by Mr Abbas."

"He was bleeding," added Hassan.

"Bleeding!" wailed Maryam's mum.

"Uncle Zaid and Uncle Hamza have gone to the big house." Umer said.

"What for? Why have they gone?" All the events began to pound Zaynab's mind.

"Tell us why," Ruqaiya shouted.

"Because Abrar and his mum are still there, and Mr Nasser fears they may get hurt," Hassan blurted out.

"So Uncle Hamza and Uncle Zaid have gone to help?" asked Zaynab.

"Yes," said Umer.

Zaynab took a deep breath. She needed to focus on getting the girls out of the harbour and home safely. *What if there were men there, those that had caused trouble in the past? What would these women do?* Zaynab thought of her daughter. A hard stern expression gripped her face: she was ready to face anyone who came in the way of her getting her daughter back safely.

"Come on. There are no lights near the beach. It's already getting dark," said Ruqaiya, who noticed every place where there was or wasn't electricity, as her old home had none. Ruqaiya abandoned Halima's arm and it hung limp as she walked forward. The boys took the lead as they knew all the short cuts and easier routes. Zaynab and Ruqaiya kept pace but Halima was struggling to keep up. She realized as she lagged behind that she needed to shake herself out of her weeping which now appeared pathetic to her too and it hindered her speed.

The daylight was abandoning them slowly. Umer led them down little paths which had just been used by animals. The women did their best to avoid the dry and wet dung littered on these paths. He then led them through people's backyards, ignoring any women who may be chasing hens and chicks, a daily ritual at this time of the day. A few people saw the group move hastily but did not object as they saw Zaynab and Halima with them. These people sensed something was wrong. They reached the fields and the group ran with speed, even Halima managed to keep up with the rest.

✎ ✎

On the very outskirt of the western side of Tobay, two great friends laughed and talked about days gone and those to come. The tide was drifting in slowly and the sand was losing its golden appearance. Both men were relieved to have seen Khalil take their news so well but something niggled away at their consciences. They should be feeling at ease but neither one of them shared their apprehension with the other. Their memories they spoke of provided a little distraction to these uneasy feelings. They walked at a steady pace with only their own movements and a few insects buzzing around them. Distant noises, which each man could not quite identify, broke their peaceful walk. Ibrahim suddenly paused and looked behind him. He saw five figures walking towards them.

"Who could they be?" Abdullah wondered.

"I think they need us. Let's walk back a little." Ibrahim sensed something untoward.

"It looks like Hamza and Zaid," he said as the blurred images became clear.

"With Nasser! What's going on?" exclaimed Abdullah.

Both men waited a few minutes for the group to reach them.

Zaid spoke first, "*Assalamu'alaykum*." Zaid noticed their anxious facial expressions. "Don't worry, Nasser is with us."

"*Wa'alaykum as-salam*. What is going on?" asked Ibrahim. Ibrahim and Abdullah looked at Nasser's wound and the bundles of luggage and immediately knew what was going on. Nasser avoided eye contact, he felt embarrassed especially in front of Ibrahim. Nasser's wife kept her head down, she too felt ashamed and guilty. She also felt pity for her husband having to face these men under such circumstances after years of hostility towards them. She held on to Abrar's arm for comfort and security and walked a few yards away from the men. She looked at her husband and saw the wound again. Relief replaced her feelings of shame, she was glad to be away from Abbas.

"Let's keep walking back to the village." Hamza was extra cautious; he didn't want anyone to see them.

"Nasser no longer works for Abbas and he needed help to get his family out, so we helped." Zaid said as plainly as he could. "We took the longest route back as it's not used that much, so no one saw us." For hours Zaid had abandoned his incessant head-touching and these few hours had brought about a change that Ibrahim, Abdullah and Hamza noticed. Zaid now spoke with poise and fortitude and at the moment seemed to be the central speaker in the dynamics of this group. Ibrahim and Abdullah glanced at each other.

"Very good. No one else is hurt are they?" questioned Abdullah.

"No, no, but there is another problem," said Zaid.

"Look!" shouted Hamza, as he pointed across the fields where Zaynab and the others were walking in the other direction. Umer could be seen leading the way. Three women in brightly coloured clothes moved swiftly, holding their long shawls over their bodies as they raced through the fields. Ibrahim noticed Zaynab, she looked taller than the rest even at that distance. Her movements came across as alien to Ibrahim, even though she was the closest person to him: there was aggression in her body language and she appeared to be oblivious of those around her, or so he perceived.

"What on earth is going on? There's Umer and his mother, and the others. Where are they going?" called out Ibrahim, confused by the sight of his wife walking so briskly.

"They look like they're in a rush. My wife is there too, I can see her," said Abdullah, totally confused and worried. Abdullah stood with his hands on his hips and gazed at the sight of the women as they ran and walked through the fields. Nasser could not bear the thought of them pausing for a second longer. He pulled at Zaid and cocked his head with a raised eyebrow. Zaid became impatient with his friends too.

"Brothers! Listen! There's a problem I was about to tell you...." said Zaid.

"Yes, and there's a problem there too. They seem to be agitated," interrupted Ibrahim, pointing towards the group of women.

"Please Ibrahim, listen! There could be real danger," said Zaid.

"They're going towards the beach," said Abdullah.

"Oh no, let's turn back. Come on, now!" Zaid pulled Ibrahim's arm.

"They could be in danger! Listen to Zaid!" Hamza spoke with a raised voice.

A new emotion sprang to life in Ibrahim and Abdullah: fear for their families began to grow in them and it began to churn in their guts with intensity.

The men started to run towards the harbour.

"Tell us on the way," said Abdullah.

Zaid started to tell them as they ran.

Nasser wanted to go with them. He looked at his wife and saw the worry on her face. He gave her a reassuring smile and picked up the bundles that Zaid and Hamza had dropped on the ground and gave them to Abrar. Tears fell from her eyes and Nasser felt awful. "Are you going after them?" she asked.

"It's the least I can do. I'm sorry for putting you through all this."

"Just be careful. I'm glad we're away from that place."

"Abrar, you know this village. Take your mother and the bags. Go to the *masjid*. Take care of your mother. Go!" Nasser took a few backward steps and turned and sprinted towards the men. Abrar and his mother walked quickly and stuck together. They were both proud of Nasser.

The men ran as fast as they could and even faster when Zaid told them about Abbas's sinister plan.

"Look, stop! You men go ahead, me and Abdullah will go to the mothers," instructed Ibrahim.

"That's fine. Be careful ," called out Hamza.

"Make *dhikr* everyone!" shouted out Ibrahim.

The men were praying for Allah's help as they ran, and their minds thought of ways to prevent the calamity taking place, while their hearts were filled with fear, fear of what could happen if Abbas's plan should be carried out.

The women had never walked so fast in their adult lives. Their legs and feet ached, especially Zaynab's and Halima's. On this frenzied journey to the harbour all sorts of small twigs and thorns had pricked their ankles and pierced their slippers as they stepped over bushes. Zaynab had actually torn her sleeve on a long rusty nail that protruded from an old farmyard gate. Ruqaiya's long hair, which she plaited, had become loose and strands were sticking out from under her shawl. Halima looked the worst. The thick line of *kohl* she applied to her eyes were now grey smudges down her cheeks and her red eyes and wet nose made her look even more distressed. All sorts of thoughts went through their minds but images of their daughters were like shadows that they were chasing. Their hearts were filled with desperate prayers for their children.

"Oh Zaynab! How could this be!" wailed Ruqaiya.

"Haven't we taught anything to our daughters? About safety? About responsibility? If my husband finds out there will be trouble," said Halima anxiously.

"*Insha' Allah* we'll find the girls. Just keep praying and moving," instructed Zaynab. Each woman blamed herself. Maybe they were lax in teaching their daughters about safety, but this was not true. Each mother tormented herself with her own silent words which increased their mental agony yet each was helpless to stop it. Their self-condemning questions like *why didn't I check on her in the afternoon?* spoiled the eloquence in the prayers they were uttering under their breaths.

Maghrib was closing in on them, as the sky became a damson canopy. The night insects had already emerged from their hidden homes. The farms and hillocks were peaceful, there was no longer any movement or sounds from the animals. The evening became cooler, the faint smell of burning firewood wafted through the village as the women of Tobay began cooking on their stoves at the back of their homes. Visibility was reducing with every passing moment, especially in this area where there were no electrical lights, and huge trees with thick, overhanging branches, lunged upwards and outwards. The darkness perturbed the women, especially as the nearby trees appeared to be moving with them. Umer and Hassan were not afraid of the dark at all. Zaynab looked at them and remembered when she was young and afraid of the dark, and all the superstitious stories her grandma would tell her in order for her and her sisters never to go out after sunset. Perhaps she should have inoculated some of these fables into Ayesha, she said to herself, going against her own reasoned mind.

The group were unaware of the men on the other side of the field. However Hassan's wandering eyes caught sight of Ibrahim and Abdullah, climbing over a steep bank.

"Look! There is your father." Hassan pointed over to the men; his outburst was aimed at Umer. The group looked over to the men. Ibrahim tried to make eye contact with Zaynab, to read her thoughts through her expressions but they were too far from them. Anyhow he could sense that she did not want to look at him directly. Perhaps his wife's actions and the predicament they were in was a culmination of his refusal to stand up to Abbas.

Although she had seen them, Zaynab could not waste any time waiting for them. A mother's love and concern drove her on. "Hassan, you run over to them and tell them what's going on. Tell them to come to the harbour. Be careful son!" Zaynab stroked Hassan's head and then began to run.

Umer and the other women followed. Hassan dashed over the bushes and headed for his uncles. Ibrahim and Abdullah were shocked to see their wives running in the opposite direction, ignoring their presence. *Do they know about it too?* Abdullah thought to himself.

"There is no power or strength except by the will of God" said Ibrahim aloud. "Things appear to be getting out of control. Why are the women running?" Ibrahim had never seen his wife run so fast. Any importance the men had, appeared to be insignificant compared with the zeal with which the women moved. Neither of the men realised that things were about to get much worse.

Hassan's physical prowess proved useful as he reached the men in hardly any time.

"Uncle Ibrahim," said Hassan, panting but strong-voiced. "Something has happened."

"Get on with it boy!" shouted Abdullah.

"Ayesha, Maryam, Fatima and Hafsa have played a dare game, meant for me and Umer......."

"Just say it!" shouted Abdullah again.

"They're hiding in the harbour, inside the boats, we think the big ones! They are waiting for me and Umer to find them!" Hassan blurted out in a single breath.

Both men were gutted. If they had ever experienced real fear before it was nothing compared to the emotional frenzy that was punching against their minds and *imaan* at this moment. They were being tested to their limits, so they thought.

"Allah, Allah Oh The Everlasting, Oh The Sustainer of Life." Ibrahim felt pain in his body, so did Abdullah. The men could not bear to think of their children in danger, fatal danger. All of them ran towards the harbour.

"No uncles! Listen! This way! It's quicker!" Hassan shouted as he pointed to where Umer was. "Trust me! I know this is a quicker route!" Hassan leapt in front of them and bolted over a small bush. The men followed, with equal vigour and fatherly fear.

CHAPTER SEVEN

The Final Game

PAST the creek, along the beach, the sand disappeared under the rippling waves as the tide came in. Patches of violet and crimson clad the sky as the orange sun began its retreat into its secret haven. The boats, small and large, made unusual shapes with their shadows, and the occasional rattle and scrape could be heard from somewhere in the harbour. The smell of fish mingled with the scent of salty sea water.

The girls were thrilled and excited as each of them chose a boat to hide in. Fatima sat in the largest one, which she chose out of her longing for a big house. She scrambled inside and hid under a seat. Footsteps drew closer. *Maybe Umer and Hassan are here*, thought the girls. The sound of walking, rather slowly and creepily, did not scare any of the girls at all. Ayesha peered out of a glass panel on the side of the boat. All she could see was the blackening ocean and darkening sky. The sound of the footsteps ceased. The girls heard a strange noise.

Maryam wondered what it was. She realised it was a container lid being unscrewed. Then came the sound of splashing. Splashing and more footsteps.

They must have come together, thought little Hafsa. More splashing could be heard then the sound of trickling as whatever was being splashed was finding its way into every indent and corner in the boats. *Very strange,* thought Fatima. The footsteps grew fainter and eventually stopped. *They must be playing it differently today,* thought Maryam. Finally the trickling sound stopped too. With innocent excitement still bubbling inside the girls, they waited patiently. Now the smell reached them. A strange, unfamiliar smell. Probably from the splashing. *What's that?* they thought. How on earth would these girls know what this smell was? It was the smell of petrol. Every single boat had been doused in petrol. Ayesha, Fatima, Maryam and Hafsa were inside them.

Was it just a coincidence that all the parties reached the harbour at the same time or did their *duas* take them there faster? They all glanced at each other for a moment and then looked at the cluster of boats. The mothers still did not know about Abbas's plan, but it soon dawned on them. The nauseating smell of petrol consumed Maryam's mother. She caught a glimpse of a spark amidst the boats. Halima fell into a heap on the muddy shore; as she fell she saw something hover over the water: *Not the angel of death, not the angel of death,* she said to herself. Suddenly she became unconscious.

The boats were alight with raging, bolting flames, flaring up into the open sky.

"Ya Allah!" screamed Zaynab.

The menacing flames spread like a drop of ink in water and the whole harbour was alight and burning. The inferno began to attract people.

Nasser bolted forward into the seething flames.

"No! You can't go!" shouted Ibrahim.

"It's the least I can do!" Nasser darted past the crowd.

"Get the women back! We'll go in!" Ibrahim pushed his son towards the women.

Racing through plumes of smoke and fumes, Nasser headed for the largest boat; Ibrahim went for the one next to it; Abdullah went for the furthest one; and Hamza and Zaid went for the nearest ones. By this time the girls were frantic. They may not have recognised the smell of petrol but they knew the smell of burning! They began to scream and howl.

The crowd watched in total and utter shock. Every single soul there prayed for Allah's help and protection. Zaynab asked for a miracle.

Hassan had an idea. "I'll go back to the village for more help!" he told Umer, and dashed out of sight. At last Hassan was showing a sense of responsibility.

Luckily, the boats the girls chose were not directly anchored to the harbour; they were in the second row. The men began their rescue attempt. The smoggy fumes burnt their nostrils as they jumped onto the boats. Hamza and Zaid bolted back from the nearest boats, as there was no way into them. They tried the ones behind them. Hamza fell as he jumped inside. Pain hammered his left knee as he smashed it on a beam. But then he saw Maryam huddled in a corner.

"Quickly Maryam!" He grabbed her by the arm and jumped out of the boat.

Zaid scurried onto the back of the next boat and saw Hafsa crouched beneath the nets.

"Hafsa!" he shouted. He stretched out for her arm and whipped the little girl out. Streaks of flames were approaching that boat. Zaid pushed her into the sea and then jumped himself.

Nasser's hair was singed and his clothes were charred but he continued to check all the compartments of the boat. The air was almost opaque but Fatima's cries led him to her. "Come here!" he yelled. She came forward and he wrenched her by the arms. Then they both jumped into the water as the boat almost exploded into a destructive inferno.

On another of the boats, Ibrahim scoured the decks, literally on his hands and knees. With both arms and hands slightly burnt he searched two of the boats. He was frantic because he had not found anyone. He did not want to leave that particular boat but he jumped off. His wounds stung in the water and then he felt numb, but he continued to swim out of the black and red fury of the burning ocean.

"*Al-Hamdulillah*! *Al-Hamdulillah*!" cried Ruqaiya and Zaynab. Nasser, Zaid and Hamza dragged the girls out of the water. Khalil and some other men went up to them to give help.

"By Allah! Are they well?" asked Khalil.

The girls lay in the women's arms. Maryam and Fatima were shivering and sobbing quietly. Hafsa was screaming in her mother's arms, who had just regained consciousness moments ago.

"Where's Ayesha? Where's Ibrahim?" Zaynab began to cry aloud.

"Don't worry. They'll come out. We need to get these children to a doctor," said Zaid.

"We need to get further back, the boats may spit fire or explode!" called out Hamza.

"Move back! Move back everyone!" shouted Khalil.

Nasser carried Maryam; Hafsa was carried by her mother; and Ruqaiya carried Fatima. Zaynab dragged herself, heavy-legged and worried, away from the blazing harbour.

Ibrahim emerged out of the water. "Ayesha! Ayesha! Is she here!" He scanned the crowd to spot his daughter.

Zaynab ran to him. "Where's Ayesha?" she screamed.

Umer watched his parents in utter fear and regret. His mother and father no longer looked strong and confident. He began to pray. Then he heard his parents pray. A sudden burst of hope went through Umer. Through the dingy air Abdullah appeared, he was hobbling and carrying a limp body in his arms. Abdullah, always so strong never looked so scared nor so small. This moment hung in the air, as though time was suspended. Every single person, standing, sitting or lying down, looked at the small lifeless figure he carried. Abdullah halted as he came near Ibrahim and Zaynab.

Zaynab let out a cry and fainted. Ibrahim, who was a man, a husband, a father, a teacher, and a believer, in his anguish called out to Allah. He held out his arms. "Give me my daughter. Give Ayesha to me." Not a single tear escaped from Ibrahim's eyes while Abdullah's tears were streaming. Ibrahim took hold of his daughter and looked at her face. It was bruised and wet. She was cold and pale. He held her close for a few moments that seemed like hours.

The harbour was eerily quiet now. Everyone was silent and the noise from the burning faded into the background as everyone's attention was riveted on the tragedy being played out before them. As Ibrahim held Ayesha close, he felt the faint beat of her heart. Ibrahim shook her gently and suddenly she coughed and made choking noises. There was a sigh of relief from everyone. Ayesha was alive.

"*Al-Hamdulillah*," whispered Ibrahim as tears began to stream down his face. The crowd gathered around them and Ibrahim laid Ayesha on the sand. She was still unconscious. Ibrahim recited *Surah al-Fatiha* seven times over her.

Meanwhile, Jameela, Hamza's wife, had come to the beach and she attempted to revive Zaynab.

"Zaynab! Zaynab! Wake up!" Jameela rubbed Zaynab's face and hands. Eventually Zaynab woke up.

"Ayesha," she whimpered.

"She's alive! She's going to be alright, *Insha' Allah*." Jameela was uncertain about Ayesha's full recovery.

Behind them the boats crackled and roared as the fire devoured them. Zaid went to Khalil. "Is there anything we can do to these boats?" he asked.

"Nothing. The petrol will burn them out completely. But I'll try to release the anchor ropes if they're not already burnt."

"Let the boats drift away," said Hamza.

"Good idea. No point in having them here. Take care Khalil, be careful you don't get hurt."

Some of the other men went forward to help Khalil.

Zaid turned to the crowd. "Everyone go home now! And keep your children indoors!" Everyone obeyed, and drifted back to their homes.

Ibrahim tried every incantation but Ayesha was in a deep sleep. Zaynab held her. "Ibrahim she needs a doctor. Someone fetch one from the town."

"Zaid, you come with me. We'll take my horse cart," said Abdullah.

"Thank you brothers," said Ibrahim gratefully.

"Please ensure that my wife and daughters are safe," Abdullah said to Ibrahim.

"Yes, we'll all go to my house," said Ibrahim as he picked up Ayesha.

"Right Umer! Help your aunties. Take them to our house and don't you dare wonder off!" He shouted at his son.

"Yes father."

The group dispersed and the *imam*, walking with Hassan who had gone to call for him, caught sight of them; he had missed all the events at the harbour.

"By Allah! I heard what happened. Hassan came to tell me. Is everyone alright? Is anyone hurt?" he asked Hamza.

"Only Ayesha, they're taking her back home. Abdullah and Zaid have gone to the town to fetch the doctor," said Hamza.

"May Allah help her. You seem to be hurt too. And you as well, Nasser." He scanned their injuries.

"Imam, is my family safe?" asked Nasser.

"Of course. We never abandon our friends. Now what are you men doing here?" The *imam* asked.

"We just stayed behind," said Hamza, as the group of men watched the floating furnace drift away into the ocean.

"That is what this village has been doing for the past few months. By passively watching what has been going on in this village you've all stayed behind. Do you not intend to go the police with this matter? To get justice? Or just watch the flames?" The *imam* spoke with determination.

"We must Hamza. Abbas planned to burn the whole harbour in daylight while people were still around. We can't let him get away with it!" Nasser was angry and defiant.

"The children suffered this time because of your complacency and lack of courage to do what was right. Not just you two but all the good men in this village. It's up to the strong ones to do something not the weak ones.

Now you must do something!" The *imam* realised that his beloved students, Umer and the others, could have been killed here tonight. Even his friends could have been killed while trying to save them.

"But how can we get to the city now?" asked Hamza.

"We'll sneak back to Abbas's estate. We can take a few horses and go to the city," Nasser explained.

"Imam you should come too!" Hamza urged.

"Of course! Justice needs to be done! Let's go!" The men headed for the estate discreetly.

Back at Ibrahim's house Umer and Hassan sat on the veranda and took care of neighbours bringing food and dry blankets for the children. Every time neighbours came they would not smile at the boys instead they would frown at them, as if to say *"look at what your games have done now!"* Umer and Hassan did not look or speak to each other either.

Inside the house Ayesha was still unconscious and had a very high temperature. Zaynab and Ibrahim tended to her in one room while the others were in the living area. Fatima, Maryam and Hafsa sat on a straw bed that had been brought in for them. They were wrapped in blankets. Maryam's mother sat beside them, thanking Allah for the safe return of her daughters. Ruqaiya and Jameela were in the kitchen preparing hot tea for the adults and hot milk with honey for the children.

The doctor arrived. "What a catastrophe! It's a miracle no one else was badly injured," said the doctor. Abdullah had also returned.

"Come through doctor, Ayesha is in here." Ibrahim ushered the doctor into the room. "Abdullah, you should check on the others." Abdullah went to his daughters.

"Mr Ahmed! You're burnt too. Oh dear. I'll see to the girl first." The doctor was appalled by the whole ordeal.

Zaynab was dabbing cold wet flannels on Ayesha's forehead. "She's very hot," she said. The doctor began to examine the patient. A few minutes passed before he spoke. "She has some swelling on her face. She must have fallen on it."

"Maybe there was a struggle to get her out or maybe she hit something in the water...the side of the boat or something?" said Ibrahim trying to find an answer.

"We'll never know for sure," said the doctor. He sensed that something was not right with Ayesha.

The room was deadly quiet. Zaynab kept looking at the doctor and then back at her daughter. Her body was aching from all the running she had done and her eyes and head throbbed with intense pain. Ibrahim's gaze was fixed upon the doctor. He couldn't read anything from his facial expressions or his movements. Zaynab went forward to kiss her daughter on the cheek. She moved Ayesha's head.

"Try not to move her please," the doctor's tone was tinged with unease.

Ibrahim looked at the doctor and felt confused and angry. The doctor's dark eyes, deeply set under bushy brows and his pale skin that proved he was not exposed to the sun regularly, gave no information to the onlookers. Then his expression changed. Suddenly his pale face became even paler.

"What is it?" Zaynab knew what it was.

"Oh dear! Please don't touch her!" the doctor fumbled in his bag.

Two small beads of dark blood emerged from her nostrils. In a slow steady stream they flowed gently over her lips and onto her chin. Ibrahim gasped in horror when he saw the deep crimson trickles on his daughter's face. He had seen and heard of this many times before and the result was not good.

The doctor took out a small glass thermometer, its mercury did not shine through the glass. Ibrahim wondered why he didn't use it before. Zaynab saw the thermometer and immediately put her hand on Ayesha's forehead to check it. It was clammy and cooler than before. The doctor tried to insert it into the patient's mouth but his fingers touched her cheek and felt the coldness. He dropped the glass instrument and began checking her forehead and arms and hands. She was deadly cold.

"Wrap her up! Wrap her up!" he stood over her and bent over to check her eyes. As he held the side of her face he felt a wet liquid from her ears. He removed his hand. His fingers were covered with the same redness that stained Ayesha's face.

"Ayesha!" screamed Zaynab.

"Is she alright? Tell us, is she alright?" shouted Ibrahim.

The doctor wished they would be quiet. He bent over her body and put his ear to her chest. A few seconds passed then he rushed to check the pulse on her neck and wrists. Desperation spread across the doctor's face and his fingers trembled as he tried to revive her. Ibrahim held Zaynab back as she wailed. Ibrahim looked at the doctor as he tried to resuscitate Ayesha with all his strength, whilst being careful not to break the poor girl's ribs. The doctor counted frantically as the room began filling with friends and neighbours. Everyone except the doctor was paralysed with fear and dread. Even Zaynab stopped screaming. Ibrahim held her tight. Then the doctor looked at the girl's face. He stopped moving. Her face was grey. Her eyes were open. She was dead.

Zaynab collapsed. Ibrahim let her fall. Ruqaiyah rushed to her friend. Abdullah too rushed over to Ibrahim and held him. Ibrahim could not balance on his feet. A strange sensation gripped his legs as if he had forgotten how to stand or walk. Abdullah pushed him to a nearby chair and made him sit on it. Abdullah held onto his friend like a father holding his child. Ibrahim muttered something under his breath. Abdullah knew what he said. He made the same prayer.

Ruqaiyah tried to silence her own crying with her hand over her mouth but she jerked more with grief. She didn't want to wake her friend up. She sat next to her on the floor and rocked forwards and backwards. She took part of her shawl and placed her hands underneath it in the prayer position. Her palms facing upwards for any morsel of mercy that might fall from above. She prayed and prayed. Her whispers were the only sound in the room.

The doctor made the final checks. He had never lost a patient so young. He looked at Abdullah for permission. Abdullah immediately understood the doctor's melancholy look. Abdullah nodded. The doctor took a deep breath and slowly stretched his hand towards Ayesha's face and gently closed her eyelids. Tears escaped from the doctor's eyes and water seeped from his nose.

"Shall I cover her?" his voice was faint.

"Not yet, her mother needs to see her. Can you wake her up?" Abdullah did not want Zaynab to wake up to see her daughter under a sheet.

The doctor took out a small brown glass bottle and a piece of cloth. He dabbed the contents of the bottle onto the folded cloth. He held the strongly scented cloth under Zaynab's nose. The smell permeated the room. Zaynab sighed and moaned before she woke up. For a minute she was dazed then her eye caught her daughter's face. She jolted upwards. She leant against the bed on her knees where Ayesha lay. This time she did not scream. Silent tears streamed down the woman's face. She saw the baby girl she gave birth to many years ago.

Ibrahim shared Zaynab's vision. He gently released himself from Abdullah's embrace and stood behind his wife. He knew what she was thinking, he knew how she was feeling. He sat down beside her and held her. Zaynab loosened her shawl and used it to wipe Ayesha's face. She saw the wet flannel she had been using before and reached for it. She dipped it in the bowl of water and cleaned the blood. She smiled when she saw Ayesha's clean face. She kissed her daughter's cheek. A tear fell from the mother's eye onto the daughter's pale face. Zaynab breathed heavily and Ibrahim grabbed her and she sunk her head into him before she let out a deafening groan, like she did when Ayesha was born. Ibrahim cried with his wife. So did everyone else.

The veranda was deserted except for Umer and Hassan. When Umer heard the groans he leapt up and ran inside. The girls sat motionless but Umer did not notice them. He barged into the room where his dead sister lay. He wished he hadn't come in. He frowned as he tried to make sense of what was happening, or what had happened. Abdullah put his arm around him.

"Umer, son. Ayesha has passed away." Abdullah couldn't bear to make eye contact with the boy.

Umer tried to translate each word into his own mind. *Passed away, where? Where has she passed away to? Is she coming*

back? Passed away what? Passed away, what is uncle talking about? Confusion was comforting for these few moments but it could not last. Umer caught sight of his father. Ibrahim stretched an arm out towards him.

"Come here."

Umer held his father and mother and cried.

"All of you sit down." Abdullah gently guided them to the other bed. The family sat huddled together and mother and son sobbed quietly now. Ibrahim looked at Abdullah.

"Send for the *imam*."

"Don't worry, I'll take care of everything. Shall I cover her?"

"Not yet. Let the others come in to see her."

As Abdullah left the room he whispered to Ruqaiyah, "Sister, don't leave them alone."

Abdullah stepped out of the house. He prayed for patience at this moment of trial. He prayed as he walked. He saw the *imam*, Nasser, Zaid and Hamza walking towards the house.

"Abdullah, we thought we'd let you know that we're going to the city police now;" Hamza stopped speaking when he saw his friend's face. The men were gripped with fear.

"What has happened?" asked the *imam*.

"It's Ayesha. She, she has died."

The men stood dumbfounded. The *imam* went forward to Abdullah and embraced him.

"Allah has only taken what already belonged to Him. Have patience my brother."

Zaid and Hamza leant against the wall and cried. Nasser paced with fury.

"See, he did it! Abbas has murdered someone!" Nasser spoke out of tone at this moment.

"Nasser. This is not the time or place for such comments. If you come inside with us you cannot behave in such a manner," ordered the *imam*.

Nasser was embarrassed, "Of course. I'm sorry."

"Can we go in now?" asked Zaid.

"Yes go in. I'll stay here. It's nearly *Fajr*." The coolness of the night air seamed to soothe Abdullah's grief a little.

The men moved slowly onto the veranda. Hassan met them at the door. The *imam* hugged the weeping boy. "Lead the way Hassan."

CHAPTER EIGHT

Farewell

A COOL mist arrived with dawn and remnants of ashes and a strange smell covered Tobay. Farmers were deliberately late this morning and the animals didn't seem to care. Very few people were awake. Last night's tragedy had enchanted most of the villagers into a deep slumber. Women moved spiritlessly as they attempted to ignite their stoves. Again and again women tossed the candescent logs from side to side with their long iron pokers but this mundane task, which they did day after day, year after year, was so wearisome that the twigs lost their heat and turned into delicate grey matter that gently rose into eddies and escaped into the air.

Ibrahim slept a little and then woke with a surprising jolt. He found himself on a bed in the living room. After a few moments he remembered some of the events from the night before. Stiffness seized his neck and back and the lacerations on his arms began to hurt. He removed the unfamiliar blanket and stood up. For the first time in his life he felt like an old man, the years had caught up with him as each joint in his body seemed to be riddled with pain and every muscle with stiffness. He glanced around the room. He saw Abdullah's long and broad body stretched out on some cushions on the floor beside his desk. Ibrahim wobbled forward and looked at the children's bedroom door. The grief returned and Ayesha's death was a reality again. Pain increased in his body. He wished he was lying on that bed inside that room instead of his daughter.

"Zaynab, Zaynab," he whispered to himself. He walked over to his bedroom and found Zaynab fast asleep with Umer by her side. Umer looked peaceful but Zaynab looked ill and her eyelids and lips were swollen and reddish. Her chaffed cheeks were raw pink. Tears escaped from Ibrahim's eyes. His heart was heavy to see his wife this way. Somewhere at the back of his mind he blamed himself for his daughter's death. He walked towards the window and covered a small gap of light between the curtains. *Let them sleep some more,* he said to himself. He didn't look through the window to see how things were beyond his own home. At this moment he did not have the mental or emotional capacity to think of anyone or anything other than his family. A small smile spread across his lips when he saw Umer, content and safe with his mother. Ibrahim leant forward and covered them both with a blanket and left the room.

Today would be one of the most difficult days of his life. *Allah help me, don't abandon me,* he said to himself. He sat on the bed again and rubbed his face.

"Did you get some sleep?" Abdullah was sitting at Ibrahim's desk rubbing his own stiff neck.

"Yes a little. You should have gone home Abdullah."

"I wanted to stay here with you."

"I'm grateful." Ibrahim paused and closed his eyes to help him think. "It's going to be difficult today. I have to bury my daughter..."

"Don't worry about the funeral arrangements or anything else. You take care of your wife and Umer."

"What about Umer's grandparents and aunties?"

"I have sent Zaid and Hamza to let them know. They have been travelling through the night. They'll be arriving in a few hours." Abdullah stood up and sat next to his friend.

Ibrahim noticed how haggard Abdullah looked. His complexion was faded and his hair and beard were dishevelled. Ibrahim had never seen him like this. Abdullah looked more unkempt as he was wearing Ibrahim's clothes which were too small for his large frame. Before sleeping he helped himself to his friend's clothes, as his own were damp and dirty.

"It's difficult to talk about but necessary. The *imam* will bring his wife and she along with Fatima's mum will wash Ayesha and prepare her for burial. I'm sorry but my wife is too weak emotionally to help in this matter and she needs to be with Zaynab anyhow."

Ibrahim gave a slow nod of approval. To hear about his daughter in such a detached way brought tears again to his eyes. Part of him couldn't believe what had happened but the grief was too painful to be unreal.

Hours earlier after the doctor had left, Abdullah and the other men discussed plans about the funeral. These men did this to make sure that their friend would not be burdened with anything more than what he was already going through. Zaid, Hamza and Abdullah all had the same thought that hammered away at their consciences: *if only we had got to the harbour quicker, maybe she would still be alive.* Zaid voiced this to the *imam* who replied, "Her death was destined to take place at that time and in the manner it happened. No one can go against God's plans. I know it's very difficult to lose a loved one, especially a child, but we must have hope in Allah's mercy. You know that she is in better care now. She will have peace and light until she is taken to paradise to be with Allah. Children have no account for their actions so she will sleep peacefully until resurrection. Our concern should be for those left behind, that they have the faith and patience to get through this tragedy. We need to be strong for Ibrahim, his wife and Umer."

A serene Zaynab emerged from her room. She was dressed in clean fresh clothes and a white floral shawl encased her tired face. Ibrahim stood up when he saw Zaynab enter the living room.

"Zaynab, are you alright?" there was a quiver in his voice. He walked towards her.

She smiled at him, "*Assalamu'alaykum.* I'm calmer this morning. I don't want to be hysterical again, we shouldn't grieve like that. I need to keep calm so I can spend the last few hours with Ayesha in a peaceful way. I don't want anything to ruin her peaceful funeral."

"I'm so sorry Zaynab, I wish I had done something sooner, I wish I had protected the children from the harbour."

"It's not your fault. Don't blame yourself. Just concentrate on giving our girl a good dignified funeral. That is all I want at the moment." She turned and walked away.

Ibrahim was amazed at the strength and great patience his wife was showing. He could see that she was being helped and cradled by Allah, truly the best Supporter. The verse from the Quran flowed from him in a beautiful soft tune: "Allah is with those that are patient."

Abdullah smiled at his friend, "Yes, let us all find comfort in this beautiful verse. I need to go and check on the *imam* and the others, but I'll be back soon."

✺ ✺

Hamza's wife Jameela had stayed the night too. She slept on a thin mattress in the kitchen with Ruqaiyah. These ladies only managed to sleep for a few hours prior to which their pillows had become soaked with their silent tears. They both awoke at the same time from the unusual coolness that crept into the kitchen. It made them wrap themselves with their shawls and thin blankets and huddle near the stove, the stove which Ruqaiyah was having difficulty to start. Ruqaiyah was very tired from yesterday's exertions making her movements slow as her legs were heavy and stiff. She arched her back as she walked.

"Jameela, please could you go to the well and fetch the water today?"

"Of course. You look terrible. Warm yourself up properly, I'll be back shortly." Jameela was physically more robust than Ruqaiyah. She had thick limbs and a stocky body but she moved quickly and with ease. As she left the kitchen from the back door she noticed how normal everything appeared in the garden. How odd that the garden seemed to be just as it was yesterday. The tropical birds sang their morning songs as they hopped from branch to branch. The cycle of life and nature seemed to be moving in its eternal rhythm. Yet all of Tobay was in grief.

The kitchen was in a state. Dirty cups were grouped together on tabletops and stools. The drops of stale milk and tea inside them looked grubby as tiny black beetles scoured them. The size of the kitchen was reduced by the makeshift beds in it. A heap of damp towels and flannels lay in the corner beside the blackened clothes. A faint smell of petrol hung in the air.

Ruqaiyah sat beside the stove and watched a large black pot of milky tea brew. She didn't notice Zaynab come in.

Zaynab sat next to her and stretched her hands to get some warmth.

"Oh Zaynab, I didn't know you were awake. You should get some more sleep." Ruqiayah was deeply concerned for her.

"I can't sleep anymore. I woke up and saw Ayesha in front of me. I prayed for strength and courage to get me through this day. I want to be alert and calm so I can pray properly today. Do you understand what I mean?"

"Yes I do." She put her arm around Zaynab. "I'm so sorry."

"She'll go to heaven, I know that."

"It will be a long day so you should have some tea and bread. Keep your strength up."

Ruqaiyah set about pouring tea in cups and cutting bread while Zaynab looked out of the window without speaking or moving. Ruqaiyah took a tray of tea, bread and honey into the living room and left it on a table for whoever wanted breakfast. She returned and saw that Zaynab had not started her breakfast at all.

"Come on Zaynab, drink your tea. Your family will be coming soon. You need your strength." Ruqaiyah lifted a cup of tea and a plate of bread and gave it to her friend.

"Say *bismillah* and eat."

It was nearly midday and the house was full with Ayesha's grandparents, uncles, aunties, cousins, other relatives, friends and neighbours. There were not enough seats so Jameela and Ruqaiyah had laid out large cotton sheets on the floor for mourners to sit on. Zaynab sobbed gently in the warm and soothing embrace of her mother and sisters. They sat together. Halima sat close to them avoiding eye contact, she wanted to cry louder but restrained herself. Her daughters were beside her with Fatima. The girls had wrapped shawls that were far too long around their heads and they sat in silence with their heads down. They didn't want to look up to see all the different people with long sad faces. If they looked up they would notice for sure that their beloved friend Ayesha was not with them. A humming noise emanated from the room as mourners prayed. Some muttered away quietly, others read from the Quran. A few people had rosemary beads which they moved through their fingers as they called out to Allah by one of His many names, 'Oh Most Gracious, Oh Most Merciful."

The veranda housed about twenty men. Ibrahim did not sit next to his father or father in law or any of his relatives. He stood beside the trellis and banister and greeted mourners as they entered with a faint and sad welcome. He had not seen some of his relatives for years. They didn't mind his aloofness, it was to be expected. He had kept his tears at bay until he saw the *imam* walk into the house carrying neatly folded white cloth. The *imam* made a quick entrance without looking at Ibrahim; he knew he would be distressed by what he held. When Ibrahim saw his daughter's shroud he held the banister so tight that his palms began to burn and sting. He cried and made a prayer for her and his family. Abdullah, who was sitting next to the elderly men on one side of the veranda, got up and stood beside his friend.

"They will perform the ritual washing now and then shroud her." Abdullah whispered to his friend, to reassure him that they were doing everything according to their religious practice.

"I know. It's the way of the Muslims. It just saddens me, I miss her already."

"You will always miss her but with patience and time it will get easier."

Khalil and Zaid exchanged looks that were not calm or befitting of a funeral. Both men felt anger at what had happened and to see their friend in such a way allowed thoughts of revenge into their minds. Nasser was too ashamed to be with the other men so he sat alone on a large rock outside the house. He broke a twig from a nearby bush and used it to draw shapes on the ground. Somehow he found it hard to pray, he just couldn't concentrate. Visions were haunting him: Abbas shouting at him, blood on his hands, running through the fields, his wife's worried expression, the smell of petrol, the orange flames, the black water, the boats, the girls, Abbas. His head hurt badly and his lacerations were still seeping a little. Mischievous flies and mosquitoes buzzed around his tasty wounds but Nasser would not let them make a feast of him.

Umer and Hassan were the only boys in the living room. They sat behind the desk. Hassan would not speak to anyone, even Umer, but he refused to leave Umer's side. He felt sad for all the times he had taunted Ayesha and he would cry every time Umer cried. Umer kept staring at his mother. He wished his grandmothers and aunties had not taken over his mother. He wanted to sit with her, feel her strong arms holding him. He wanted to cry out to his mother. He was sorry for everything. An overwhelming feeling of regret consumed him. He should have saved Ayesha, he should have done something.

His grief was tormenting him. *Ummi, Abu.* He just wanted to be with his parents.

Fatima and Maryam looked up at the wrong time. They saw the *imam* hand over the white cloth to his wife. This puzzled Fatima.

"What's that?" she whispered in Maryam's ear.

"That is a shroud. It is clean white cloth. They will wrap Ayesha in it."

"What for?"

Zaynab's sister overheard and whispered to the girls: "Ayesha will be going to meet Allah so she needs to be clean and ready."

"But she's always clean," remarked Fatima, recollecting the daily bathing Zaynab would enforce on her children.

"Fatima dear, can you remember what your teacher taught you about what the Prophet (peace be upon him) said about cleanliness?"

Fatima tried to think but struggled to make any mental connection. Maryam looked up, she remembered what Madame had taught them.

"Maryam can you remember?"

"Yes aunty. He taught us to be clean and pure and that cleanliness is part of our faith."

"Well done, you're right. Our religion teaches us to be clean. As Muslims we wash our hands before we eat, we make...."

"Make *wudu* before we pray!" interrupted Maryam.

"Yes we wash before we pray our five daily prayers, again showing that cleanliness is very important."

"But what is the cloth for?" Fatima was still puzzled.

"Even when we die we must be pure and cleansed from any dirt that may be on our bodies. Allah expects His believers to be clean when they return to Him in the hereafter."

"Aunty will they give her a bath?" asked Maryam.

"It's called a *ghusl*. A few people will give her a wash making sure she is clean. They may put fragrance on her to make her smell nice. Finally they will carefully wrap her in the white cloth, the shroud."

"Why is it white aunty?" asked Fatima now fully immersed in the conversation.

"The blessed Prophet recommended that the shroud be white."

"So is everyone's shroud white?" asked Maryam.

"It should be white for everyone, rich and poor, young and old, boy or girl. It shows that we are all equal before Allah, only a person's good deeds will bring them closer to Allah."

"She was a good girl," said Maryam in a quiet voice.

"Yes she was." Tears streamed down the lady's face. She reached out and put her arms around both girls. She whispered to them, "There is something I forgot to tell you. Do you know that Allah is so Kind and Merciful that when children die they are not judged the way in which adults are, but instead they all go to heaven. So when you're feeling sad remember that Ayesha has gone to heaven, the very best of places."

Maryam thought of her dear friend, her best friend. Who would she play with now that Ayesha had passed away? She remembered reading with her and playing with their dolls together. Hafsa was too shocked by the fire at the harbour to even understand that Ayesha was dead. She didn't even know why they were at Ayesha's house. Shock and fright made her mind blank. She sat clutching her mother's arm, her oversized headscarf covering most of her sullen face and droopy eyes.

The *imam's* wife and Ruqaiyah appeared. Ruqaiyah approached Zaynab. She looked at Zaynab's mother and nodded. Zaynab looked up at the standing ladies. It was time. Zaynab's mother sat straight and took a deep breath. A serious expression covered her wrinkled face. She held Zaynab's arm firmly and said: "It's time Zaynab. It's time to say goodbye to little Ayesha."

CHAPTER NINE

Confrontation

AFTER the funeral Zaynab fell asleep in her room. Her mother and sisters encouraged her to get some rest. They called for Umer and asked if he wanted to be with his mother. He wanted to but the loyal Hassan would not leave his side so they both perched on the bed and fell asleep next to Zaynab.

Walking back from the cemetery Ibrahim felt much calmer. Abdullah and the *imam* had led the funeral procession through the village to the small cemetery. Now Abdullah was feeling very tired but relieved that it was all over. The men dispersed, some went to their own homes, and others went to their farms. Ibrahim's relatives followed him to his home but Zaid, Hamza, Khalil and Nasser lingered behind. Abdullah and the imam looked back and saw the men huddle close together and talk. They knew what they were discussing.

"You make sure that Ibrahim and the visitors are taken care of. I'll see to them. When you're ready we'll meet at your house," said the *imam*. He turned and went over to Zaid and the others. Abdullah realised that it would be a very long day.

The men anticipated that the *imam* would join them. Imam Abdurrahman was the only one that was calm although he was grieving too. The other men tried to contain their anger, their heavy breathing and serious expressions showed they were seething with the desire for revenge.

"We're on our way to the city to tell the police. This time its murder and we can't and will not let Abbas get away with it!" said Zaid.

"Of course not. We should have approached the police a long time ago," replied the *imam*.

"Well no one wanted to support me when I wanted to go," reflected Hamza.

"Let's concentrate on getting there quickly. I feel that Abbas may abscond, he must have heard the news. If Abbas gets away he'll be hard to find," said Nasser, who knew how Abbas would react to such a situation.

"Yes, and he'll probably bribe people to maintain his safety. You don't think he would bribe the police? We hear of these things don't we?" asked Khalil.

"Let's pray that we come across police with integrity and principles," said the *imam*.

"We should talk on the way. We'll take Abdullah's horses. Hurry up,"ordered Zaid.

Farmers out in the fields halted and watched the group of men ride through the dusty lane out of Tobay. The observers nodded their heads with approval and some envied them, they wanted to join them. Nasser rode the fastest. He ignored the pain in his body and refused to be distracted. Pangs of hunger and tiredness were another test for them, they had not had breakfast and their wounds had not been seen to. Nevertheless they rode well and the horses made good time. A huge cloud of smoky dust danced in their wake and made everyone who saw it tremble a little with awe. Finally the men were out for justice.

It took about an hour to reach the city and the winding lanes that passed through busy little markets made them slow down. The heat seemed to be more ruthless here too. The men were covered with perspiration and the flies and mosquitoes followed the newcomers with speed. Despite the festoons of colour and aromas that filled the bazaar, from stalls selling exotic fabrics to those selling spices and herbs, the men were not interested in the frequent invitations from shop sellers. *I will give you a good price for this my dear friend,* the men at the stalls would say, with shiny bronze skin and yellow teeth. The men rode on until they reached the police station.

They left their horses and went inside. They allowed the *imam* to go in first. His attire and calm demeanour was an indication of his position in the community. Even the police, however corrupt, paid special respect to religious leaders. After speaking to a couple of junior officers the group was led to another room with seats around a large desk. A few papers were piled to one side and an ink font and clock were the only other items on it. The men waited patiently. It was stuffy and the faint smell of body odour made it worse. It was poorly ventilated and the electric fan on the ceiling moved its rusty blades so slow that the flies sitting on them did not move. A few old picture frames of ancient-looking officers were the only decoration on the wall. The men sat in silence and each was glad they had not brought Ibrahim with them.

A middle-aged man walked in and sat opposite them. He looked tired and worried. The *imam* began his story. The others listened and hoped that the policeman in front of them would bring them justice. The senior officer nodded and made occasional notes. The *imam* came to the end of his case.

"We want retribution. The little girl's life has to be paid for in some way," was the *imam's* closing statement. The *imam* wiped his face and swallowed hard. He was dehydrated and his mouth and throat were dry.

The senior office scanned the men and nodded.

"I'm amazed that you men did not come to see me before. How can good men of the community let this happen?"

This did not make them feel better.

"Do you have such little faith in us? That we would not do anything? Could you not foresee that a dangerous man, one who is so treacherous like this Abbas character, could bring about physical harm to you and your families? I have seen men from villages take on some evil brutes for the right reason. What kept you back?" The senior officer was not impressed with this group of men, however gallantly they rode to get there.

Abdullah spoke. "Abbas had threatened some of us with violence to our property and to our families. We couldn't take the risk."

"I see, but he got away with doing whatever he pleased. In summary; he has ruined the boats that belonged to poor yet honest fishermen as he could not force them to rent his boats. And he also burnt his own boats to punish the ones that had rented the boats, as they had not urged their fellow fishermen to do the same! This man is utterly ruthless!"

"We have heard that some policemen, not from this station, but heard in general that police often take bribes from criminals," said Zaid.

The senior officer stood up. "Those that take bribes don't deserve to be policemen. I know what you have heard. I have had the misfortune of dealing with corrupt police officers in this very station. It's evil and a kind of greed I think that makes a man sell his principles. But rest assured I'm not like that nor are my officers."

The men sighed with relief. A tiny tear escaped from the *imam's* eye. Justice would be done.

The senior officer banged hard on the table top a few times and three officers came in.

"Have you heard everything?"

"Yes sir!" they replied.

"Then get the horses ready and the prisoner cart. Get the rifles and a box of cartridges. Quickly!"

"Yes sir!"

"Rifles, will that be necessary?" asked the *imam*.

"Of course! Do you not think that this crazy man Abbas has a gun or a rifle?"

"Actually he does. It's best if you defend yourselves," said Nasser.

"As police we always do and I never want to put my officers at risk."

The men waited outside while the police officers got ready. The *imam* was the most nervous. He thought there had been enough violence and bloodshed and he hated the use of any weapon. Abdullah and the senior officer led the way. Abdullah told him that the girl's father was his closest friend. The officer said it made no difference who the father was, the girl was murdered and the murderer needs be put away. He had children too, the officer explained.

"I am always worried about their safety, especially from criminals who swear revenge but your courage should always be greater than your fear. Remember that."

Abdullah felt relieved and rejuvenated to hear those words.

It took a little longer to reach Abbas's house as they went around the village to get to it. Nasser led them into the compound. An officer ordered the men not to go inside with them. The senior officer accepted Nasser's plea to assist them. Abdullah and the others watched from beside the prisoner cart. The *imam* was unsettled to see the officers run up the garden leading to the main house with their black rifles and handguns.

"It's courageous of Nasser to go in with them," said Hamza.

"He knows the house and where to find Abbas. I hope Abbas hasn't already run off," said Zaid.

"He needs to be put away for what he has done. Ibrahim has suffered so much," said Abdullah.

"Where is everyone? I thought Abbas had lots of workers. I can't see anyone," Khalil noticed the emptiness of the place.

Abbas had not received the news until late that morning. He sat at his breakfast table and as usual relished in a large breakfast. His servant trembled a little as he cleaned the table. The crockery clanked in his hands. The servant knew what had happened and did not want to be near the man who was responsible for it.

"Send Tariq in," he ordered.

"Yes sir," replied the servant.

Tariq was already at the door. He entered without seeking permission. His appearance was untidy and Abbas's grave expression made him frown and sweat a little.

"You look disgraceful," remarked Abbas in a calm tone. He reached for a cigarette from a wooden box nearby.

"Something very bad has happened. Very bad."

"Good. That's what I wanted to hear. Teach that lot a lesson I hope." Abbas smoked and walked around the room.

"No sir. It's not good at all. Someone was killed last night."

"Killed. A poor fisherman. One who couldn't pay for his boat. Who will miss such a decrepit person?" Abbas was not moved at all. Tariq began to think if Abbas had killed anyone before as he didn't seem to care at all. Abbas was immune to the seriousness and gravity of this news.

"Sir, someone was killed. I did it. You did it. Do you not feel remorse sir?" Tariq stood facing his master.

Abbas noticed that Tariq was serious and defiant. "Well it's done. You don't worry about it. Just take your bonus and don't mention it to anyone. No one has proof anyway. Your bonus is on the desk." Abbas returned to his armchair and continued smoking his cigarette without making eye contact with Tariq.

Tariq sighed heavily and turned to leave the room. As he left he said "A little girl has died. Ibrahim's daughter."

Abbas couldn't believe what he heard. He turned to look at Tariq but he had already left and the sound of him running down the hallway could be heard. Abbas paused in his actions and recollected those words again. A peculiar emotion entranced him.

"Ibrahim's daughter is dead. Killed because of me," he whispered to himself. The heaviness of guilt weighed him down, further into his seat. *What have I done? This is very bad.* He looked around the room in confusion. He saw the bundle of money on the desk. Things did not look good for him. He jumped out of his seat and looked out of his window. He saw what he suspected from the abandoned bundle of money. Tariq was on horseback riding out of the compound. Abbas felt frightened and alone. His power, wealth and everything he had built seemed to be crumbling around him. As he brought the cigarette to his mouth he noticed his hand was shaking. He knew he was in trouble. Deep trouble. The village might have been reluctant to stand up against him because of the boats but they would never turn a blind eye to murder. Ibrahim and his friends would surely avenge the girl's death.

He threw the cigarette on the floor and stomped on it hard. Pacing around the room he thought of his options. *I'll leave Tobay and set up home elsewhere.* But leaving would not be easy and setting up home elsewhere was even more difficult. *What shall I do?* With no friend or relative to turn to and no place to go his thoughts fell upon the contents of the cupboard in the corner of the room. *I must prepare myself, I don't know what these villagers may do.* He opened up his cigar and cigarette box and emptied it onto his desk. Carefully he removed the wooden tray that held them and took out a small dirty brass key that was hidden beneath it. He rubbed the key gently and opened the cupboard. On the top shelf was a wooden box. His hands trembled as he reached for it. Sitting behind his desk he opened it and removed the cold object from its cloth wrapping. Abbas was unsure of how to use it properly. It had been decades since he last used it. He opened the barrel and found it wasn't empty. *This should be enough,* he reassured himself but deep inside he knew he was wrong, wrong for everything he had done. Abdullah and Ibrahim would never forgive him but he wasn't sure he wanted their forgiveness either. At this moment he needed to be ready for anyone who might confront him. He would use the handgun if he was forced to.

Abbas waited behind his desk for hours. The servant did not knock on his door to bring in late morning tea or lunch. The house was silent. The compound was silent.

When they saw Tariq leave in haste they decided to do the same. They bundled their few belongings in sacks and took what they needed from the compound and left. First Nasser had left and now Tariq. The dozen or so workers realized that Abbas's wage, which was regular and much needed was not worth it, and despite their guilt for working for such a person, the death of an innocent girl had changed everything. The compound was lifeless and the gates to the main house and even the doors were left open. Abbas was truly alone and vulnerable to the outside world. The magnitude of his crime wrestled with his guilt but he would still not allow feelings of remorse or sympathy for those affected.

He sat and waited. His palms became sweaty and he kept wiping them on his trouser legs, he did not want the handgun to slip. His nervous eyes were firmly fixed on the open door. For the first time Abbas could feel the spaciousness of his house. Every little noise that he could hear before was gone. Only a silence that became a deafening ringing in his ears. He did not admit it, or want to acknowledge it, but a voice from somewhere in his mind told him: *this is what you have become.* It sounded like his father's voice but it also sounded like Ibrahim. An unusual noise brought him out of his inner thoughts. He felt his blood pressure rise. He could feel and hear his heart beat faster. His legs tingled nervously. True fear seized him. The unidentified noises became louder as they drew nearer.

Abdullah walked towards the gate, ignoring the command of the officer who was in charge of the prisoner cart. He held the black iron gate and waited for Abbas to be dragged out of his fortress. He could still feel Ayesha's dying body in his arms. He could still taste the salt from the doomed waters and the smell of petrol was entrenched in his sinuses. He imagined Abbas being brought out like an animal. This gave him a little relief. Zaid was agitated. He wanted to go inside but held back. In his mind he went over all the things he wanted to say to Abbas. Occasionally he would twitch his face and screw his mouth up while he rehearsed his condemnation.

A shot was fired. It whistled through the air and its echo was clear and loud. The men were shocked. Abdullah looked back at the other men. The *imam* sat on a nearby rock and cupped his hands and began praying. The others joined Abdullah at the gate. They did not exchange words. They wondered what had happened. Who had fired the shot? Was anyone hurt? Did Abbas use his gun? Another shot was fired a few seconds later. And another. A junior officer ran out of the house. He stopped and blew on his whistle then waved at the officer with the prisoner cart. This was his signal to bring it to the house. The officer mounted his horse and responded to his call.

The men did not know what to do. Zaid ran past the gate and Hamza followed.

"We should wait like the officer said," called out Abdullah, but it was no use.

A few minutes passed and they could see the policemen run down the lane. Nasser could not be seen. The senior officer panted heavily when he reached them.

"What happened? Where's Nasser?" asked Abdullah.

"I'm afraid he has been shot in the leg by Abbas."

"How terrible!" gasped the *imam*.

"He knew his old boss very well. Abbas took one look at Nasser and shot him without provocation. A 'traitor' is what he called him."

"How is Nasser?" asked Abdullah.

"They're bringing him in the prisoner cart. They'll take him to the town hospital, it's nearer than the city. I'll send for another prisoner cart for Abbas."

"What about his wound? Will he be alright?" asked the *imam*.

"Yes, I should think so. I've seen plenty of wounds like that and Nasser is a strong man. He wasn't afraid to go in that room despite Abbas's threats."

"What a mess," said the *imam*.

"No, Imam Abdurrahman. We have results. Abbas is restrained and will soon be taken to the police station. He will not be going anywhere especially since he shot at a man in full view of my officers. No court is going to ignore my testimony. He'll be spending the rest of his days in the provincial prison. Mark my words."

Zaid ran back to them and as ever gave them an account of Nasser's wound and all that had happened.

"Hamza will go with him to the town hospital. Pray that he recovers," said Zaid.

"Our job here is done now, we should head back," said the *imam*.

"Yes, we need to spend time with Ibrahim now," said Abdullah.

"Me and Khalil will go to the station, if that's alright with you officer?" asked Zaid.

"Yes, we need to write up the reports for this. But I need to wait for another prisoner cart to arrive before I leave here." The senior officer sent a single junior officer on horseback back to the station.

"How is Abbas? Does he show any remorse?" asked Abdullah.

"Not really. Maybe he'll change after a few years behind bars but now he is full of hate for you all. He's blaming the death on one of his workers, a man called Tariq. We need to find him too."

"We must go now. Thank you so much for doing this. Allah will reward you for your efforts," said the *imam*.

"Yes, thank you. I feel relieved that he is no longer free. My friend will be pleased," said Abdullah.

The *imam* and Abdullah left Abbas's grounds and headed back to Ibrahim's home. They walked slowly and said very little. They were tired and their minds were filled with so much that each did not have the strength to talk. When they reached Ibrahim's house, their friend was waiting on the veranda for them.

"I heard you went to the city. What happened?" asked Ibrahim.

"We don't need to worry about Abbas anymore." Abdullah smiled as he spoke to his friend. The men sat on chairs in the shadiest part of the veranda.

"*Al-Hamdulillah*, he will be taken to prison and the senior officer assures us that he will be imprisoned," said the *imam*.

Ibrahim was relieved and the conversation was a good distraction from his grief.

"There were complications though, as usual with Abbas!" said Abdullah.

"Like what?" asked Ibrahim.

"Nasser was shot in the leg by Abbas," replied the *imam*. "But no one else was hurt and he has gone to the town hospital with Hamza. He'll be fine *Insha' Allah*."

Ibrahim closed his eyes and massaged his temple with his hand. The *imam* and Abdullah looked at each other realizing that perhaps they should not have said anything yet.

"Don't be too alarmed. The matter has been taken care of now," said the *imam*.

"I'm not alarmed. I knew Abbas wouldn't be arrested easily. He has been defiant all his life. His defiance and greed has taken my daughter's life. I wish Abbas was shot instead."

The *imam* was shocked to hear such violent words which were against all he believed in. He thought best not to say anything, after all Ibrahim had just hours before buried his daughter. Abdullah knew the *imam* would not like his friend's words.

"I admit I had that feeling too. As a father you only want justice for what happened, it's natural, and he will face a life sentence in the provincial prison especially since his aide cannot be found. The blame is entirely on him," explained Abdullah.

Ibrahim looked up at his friends. His eyes were watery and the peace and softness that had been a feature of his face was no longer there. Bereavement had stripped it away from him. He was not the Ibrahim they knew.

"My brother, you have a right to feel this way but have patience too. Ayesha is in a place far better than here. You must remain steadfast for yourself and your family. Don't let Abbas take anything else away from you. You don't want your faith to diminish because of him, or your family to become weak? We must remain certain that true justice will be seen on the Day of Judgement, and we will be rejoined with those that we love." The *imam* tried to provide comfort by reminding them of the bigger picture as seen by a believer.

Zaynab had woken up hours earlier and spent her time with her mother and sisters. She overheard everything the men had been saying and was relieved that Abbas was arrested but she too wished something more gruesome had happened to him. She felt an emptiness inside her that could not be filled or soothed. Every time she experienced this she called for Umer and held him close. She wept occasionally but spent most of her time praying. Umer joined her in her prayers and Hassan repeated whatever verse he knew to himself. The atmosphere in the house was calmer but the air felt thick and heavy with grief.

Halima joined Ruqaiyah and Jameela in the kitchen and helped prepare some tea for everyone. Fatima, Maryam and Hafsa perched themselves on a makeshift bed and kept silent throughout the day. Slowly the reality of their friend's death dawned upon them even though this realisation was only as primitive as their innocuous minds would allow. Ruqaiyah called for Hassan and he took tea out for the men on the veranda. His mischievous expression was lost and there was no colour in his once rosy cheeks. He made no eye contact with anyone in the kitchen or elsewhere. He returned to his friend who subconsciously felt his short absence and was happy with his quick return.

The house was generally quiet and most of the mourners left the house before sunset except Umer's grandparents and aunties. They would be staying for a few days to console Ibrahim and Zaynab. The night felt exceptionally dark and Ibrahim slept on the veranda hammock. He looked at the stars high above in the sky. He gazed for a long time before his fatigue finally overcame him.

Zaynab could not sleep. Her eyes were fixed on a candle that burned slowly. Its melted wax streamed slowly over its side and onto the small plate that it was fixed to. The delicate flame moved gently and flickered with a peaceful rhythm that soothed Zaynab. The painful empty pit she felt in her stomach from her longing to hold her daughter again slowly disappeared. Ayesha may be dead to the world, she thought, but she would always be her daughter and nothing would ever take that away from her. Allah had made Zaynab her mother and soon she would see her daughter again in the Hereafter. She prayed that they would be reunited in paradise and together they would be safe from all harm and danger, and they would never be separated. Zaynab comforted herself with these thoughts. This is what the imam's wife had reminded her about before she left the house. Zaynab closed her eyes and resumed her prayer and soon she was fast asleep.

CHAPTER TEN

Peace

THE first few weeks were strained and hard for everyone in Tobay despite the fact that Abbas was not around. It took many weeks for everyone to recover from the tragedy and still it was not, and could never really be, a full recovery. When people saw Ibrahim back at the school fixing the gate and Zaynab buying vegetables, the grief slowly dissipated. Umer could be seen running with Hassan in games of chase and this gave everyone who saw it an opportunity to laugh and smile. Apart from Ayesha's parents, Maryam took the longest to recover from Ayesha's death and often behaved like a mute for days on end. She was intelligent for her age but her best friend's death swept aside any understanding of life and death. She wished she would come back. Halima spent most of her days trying to be close to the silent Maryam but it was only when Maryam saw Zaynab that she felt some relief. Zaynab did her best to comfort her. Abdullah constantly told everyone that she needed to grieve in her own way and in her own time. Ayesha was her best friend and her death would obviously have a devastating effect on her.

The school needed a lot of attention but Ibrahim wanted to spend more time with Zaynab, who would occasionally spend hours staring into space in silence. He thought how he could resolve this as he couldn't bear to spend hours every day at home, the memory of the funeral was rekindled every time he sat in the living room. An idea sprang to mind. He approached Zaynab. She was sweeping the veranda with a broom with fine twigs.

"Zaynab dear, come and sit with me for a few minutes." Ibrahim sat on the wooden bench and placed his palm on the seat next to him. Without replying Zaynab rested the broom against the wall and sat beside him. Ibrahim noticed her gaunt face. Her eyes were sunken and she had lost some weight.

"Zaynab, I know you are very busy running the home but may I ask you for some help?"

"What is it?" They had not spoken at length since the funeral.

Ibrahim found her short response hurtful.

"I'm hurting too Zaynab, she was my daughter too."

Zaynab was embarrassed. Tears streamed from her eyes and she realised that her husband needed support too. "Oh, Ibrahim. I'm trying my best to see through the days but I see her face everywhere."

"You don't want to ever forget her face do you? She is your daughter and only death has separated you from her. She is our Ayesha and always will be so remember her face with happiness."

Zaynab smiled at her husband. Ibrahim seemed to have become again the man she knew before the death. His words gave her comfort and she felt the heaviness being lifted from her. She gazed ahead and saw Ayesha playing, smiling and wearing the pink dress she stitched for her. She remembered Ibrahim asking her for help.

"Ibrahim, what help do you need?"

"I wonder if you can spare some time at school? I need to get the place sorted out. It's in a real state."

Zaynab paused and Ibrahim waited patiently. She thought about the school. She always wanted to be more involved with the school. "Will it be alright if I help out?"

"Yes of course, the head teacher demands it!" Ibrahim smiled.

"When shall I come? I have lots of chores to complete today."

"Fancy coming with me now? The school has enough chores." Ibrahim stood up and walked out of the veranda.

"I'll let Ruqaiyah know. She is busy embroidering something with Abrar's mother. They're at the back." Zaynab had perked up and it was refreshing for her to be taken away from her routine activities. Ibrahim looked back and saw his wife smiling, she was waving at the neighbour as she walked onto the pathway.

Ibrahim paused beneath a large guava tree and inhaled the sweet aroma. Colour had returned to the village. He waited for Zaynab who was busy chatting to a couple of plump women. Their clothes festooned against the earthy colours of the lane. Lime, pink and orange, along with the blue shawl which was draped over Zaynab's head and shoulder. She carried a straw bag which was bulky with items. She looked happier.

"Zaynab, it's so nice to see you out of the house!" remarked one of the women who were carrying rolls of cloth.

"Yes, I'm helping out at the school today," Zaynab replied with satisfaction.

"We're so glad your husband sent that man away," said another as she bent over her basket of fruit and picked a handful of guava and mangoes.

"It wasn't actually my husband but the others." Zaynab didn't want to talk about such things especially when she felt Ibrahim had little to do with Abbas's arrest.

"Of course he did! His friends were the ones that rode out of the village to get the police. It was his friends who confronted him." The woman stood up with the fruit bundled in her long scarf.

Zaynab looked perturbed. "Ibrahim has done so much for this village. When Abbas was offering us his help Ibrahim kept warning us," remarked the woman carrying the cloth.

Zaynab knew they were right but still she had hoped that her husband had done more to put Abbas away. "Yes that is true," she replied showing that she was still loyal to her husband in every way.

Her attention fell upon the rolls of cloth the woman was carrying. She stretched out her hand and felt the different textures. "Some lovely fabric here, who is it for?"

"For me and my family."

Zaynab was taken aback. She couldn't hide her surprise. How could these women afford such fabric?

"Your husband has been to the city a few times and has urged the court to give us compensation for our boats. The money has come from Abbas's property. You must have known about that."

The women realized that Zaynab was unaware of her husband's activities. They smiled at her and she gave an awkward smile back.

"We need to go now but take this fruit and share it with your husband and anyone else at the school." The woman tipped the guava and mangoes into Zaynab's bag.

"*Jazak Allah*. It's kind of you." Zaynab though embarrassed was pleased that these women had some sort of security again.

She watched the women walk ahead and their vibrant dresses made her smile. She felt better.

Ibrahim had been watching the scene from under the guava tree but did not hear everything as three men with their carthorses passed by noisily. He wondered what had been said especially when Zaynab laughed at him and walked passed him saying "Come on Ibrahim, we've got work to do! I've got plans for Tobay School!" She hummed as she went ahead. Ibrahim followed behind.

Hassan was sitting on a sandy boulder outside the *masjid*. He held a book in his hands and was reading, straining the occasional syllable. Zaynab was impressed to see the young Hassan do something other than run around and frighten animals. Ibrahim walked ahead. Zaynab approached the well-dressed boy. "*Assalamu' alaykum* Hassan, what are you doing?"

"Aunty!" Hassan was a little flustered. "I'm learning to read, I mean I can read. My mother bought this book from the city last month." Hassan's outward appearance was unusual as he was well-dressed and his skin, teeth and nails all looked polished and fresh. Zaynab wondered if Hassan's father had been compensated too.

"Your mother went to the city?" she questioned.

"Yes, so did many others, to get things and clothes and shoes. Look!" Hassan stretched out his feet and showed off his new leather sandals. "My big brother says I'd better not ruin or lose these. They've got new shoes too and a new boat."

Zaynab kissed Hassan on the forehead. "Where is my Umer? I haven't seen him all day."

"He's gone with the *imam* to get some wood from uncle Khalil. They're making a frame. Abrar's mother has made something for the *masjid*."

"Yes, aunty Ruqaiyah is helping her too. I haven't seen what they're making."

Zaynab felt overwhelmed. It seemed to her that everyone had been busy doing things for each other and for the village. She felt optimistic and excited about going to the school.

Abdullah had brought Maryam and Hafsa to the school. The girls were in the yard. Maryam was dressed in a deep pink dress and wore a small red and white floral scarf over her head. Hafsa skipped with a thin rope while Maryam sang to her. Both girls looked joyful and content. Abdullah watched his daughters and was happy that Maryam was having one of her good days today.

"Abdullah, I didn't expect to see you here," said Ibrahim as he unlocked the main school door.

"I have cancelled your agreements with the town school. We're all glad you're staying. I thought I'd bring the girls here. Maryam has been feeling better this week. How are your wife and Umer?"

"Umer is fine but sometimes he sits quietly. I have brought Zaynab today to help out with the improvements here. She will be glad to see the girls."

When Zaynab saw the girls she had mixed emotions. Their pretty outfits made her smile but she felt the urge to cry again. The emptiness returned again, she took a few deep breaths and recited a short prayer. Maryam saw her and ran to her and flung her arms around her.

"Aunty! Have you come to help at the school?" Maryam smiled showing her cute dimples and uneven teeth.

"Yes, Maryam." Zaynab wanted to hold her for longer but Maryam pulled herself away and began jumping and rocking in a playful manner.

"Aunty, can Hafsa and I help you?"

"Of course you can. Let's walk around the school first, I need some fresh air." Maryam put her arm around Zaynab and Hafsa left the rope on the dusty ground and skipped beside them.

"My mother has a blue shawl like this one," said Maryam inspecting a corner of Zaynab's shawl.

"I gave her a similar shawl last year for *Eid*. Does she wear it often?"

"Sometimes. Aunty can Hafsa and I come to your house and play in the garden? Can Fatima come too?"

"Of course, I'd like that," replied Zaynab as she leant over and kissed her on her cheek.

They walked towards the small garden where the school children planted a few vegetables. Ibrahim saw them and walked towards them. He had something to show Zaynab.

Hafsa's hair became dishevelled and Zaynab decided to neaten it while Maryam looked around the garden. Zaynab enjoyed this activity and chatted away with the girls blissfully.

"Zaynab, I forgot to show you something." Ibrahim pointed towards a small tree growing in front of the wall. It was about three feet and its foliage was healthy and green.

"It's a nice little tree. I'm surprised it wasn't destroyed by the storm. The other plants have been damaged."

Zaynab looked at the plants and pulled her face with disappointment.

"Yes, most of the plants have been ruined but this one survived."

"It had the shelter of the wall, I suppose."

"Do you know who planted it?" asked Ibrahim, certain that the answer to this question would make her happy.

"*Abu! Ummi!*" called out Umer. Ibrahim and Zaynab stepped away from the garden and walked towards the main playground. Maryam and Hafsa ran to their father who was talking to the *imam*. Umer was standing in between the tall Abdullah and the *imam*, both clad in cool white cotton. Umer was holding a large flat object.

"What is Umer holding?" asked Zaynab.

Ibrahim knew what it was but didn't want to spoil the surprise. He smiled again, knowing that Zaynab would be glad to see what the mysterious object was. She glanced at him and saw his happy expression.

"Ibrahim, what is it?" She nudged him slightly, "Tell me."

"*Assalamu'alaykum* Ibrahim, sister," the *imam* greeted them. Umer left the small group and walked towards the garden with Maryam and Hafsa peering over his arms trying to get a glance of the mysterious object. Umer enjoyed teasing them.

Abdullah laughed and the *imam* smiled at his friends. Ibrahim looked at the children and experienced a sensation of relief and gratitude to Allah that his family and friends were safe. He took hold of Zaynab's hand.

"Zaynab, let's look at what our Umer is holding. Umer!" Ibrahim and Zaynab stood facing the garden as the girls played amongst the broken pots.

"Yes *Abu*," replied Umer hiding the object away from the vision of his mother; he knew that his father wanted him to do this.

"What are you father and son up to?"

"Firstly, look at the tree." Zaynab looked at the small tree again, confused at how it could have survived the terrible storm yet glad that it had.

"Ibrahim, didn't you have chores for me to do here?" said Zaynab attempting to cover her obvious incomprehension with what her husband was doing.

"That tree survived the powerful storm. As you can see it is the only thing that has not been destroyed, not even slightly damaged by the rain."

Zaynab was still confused. Umer had tears in his eyes. He knew the story of this tree.

"Zaynab, that tree was planted by Ayesha. Our Ayesha."

Silent tears fell from her eyes but she was smiling too. She held Umer close to her while Ibrahim took the large object and held it in front of her so she could see it. It was a picture with a brown wooden frame. Ibrahim tilted the frame as the reflected radiance from the sunshine was blurring the actual picture

"Nasser's wife has been embroidering this for days. Sister Ruqaiyah has been helping her too. The *imam* is going to place it in the *masjid* so everyone can see it. It's beautiful isn't it?"

Zaynab took the frame and held it in her view. Her tears stopped. She read aloud the words that were so carefully and beautifully embroidered on delicate fabric:

"Allah loves those who are patient and steadfast."

Glossary

Abu Father

Al-Hamdulillah All praise belongs to Allah (God).

Allah Arabic word for God used by muslims.

Allahu Akbar, Allahu Akbar 'God is Most Great, God is Most Great'.

Ameen Used at the end of a prayer asking for God's acceptance.

Asr One of the five daily prayers in Islam; the afternoon prayer.

Assalamu'alaykum Greeting of a muslim meaning; peace be upon you.

Astagfirullah I seek forgiveness from God (Allah).

Bismillah Used at the beginning of an action meaning; in the name of God (Allah).

Dhikr Remembrance of God (Allah).

Dua Prayer/Supplication

Fajr One of the five daily prayers; the morning prayer.

Hadith A report of the sayings or actions of the last prophet of Islam (Mohammed).

Hijaab Modest dress worn by muslim women covering the head and body.

Imaan Faith in God

Imam A leader of a muslim community e.g the one who leads the prayer in the masjid/mosque.

Insha' Allah By the Will of God (Allah).

Isha One of the five daily prayers; the night prayer.

Jazak Allah Arabic verbal expression to say 'thank you', meaning; may God reward you generously.

Maghrib One of the five daily prayers; the evening prayer.

Masha' Allah "As God has willed" – this phrase is used when admiring or praising something or someone, in recognition that all good things come from God and are blessings from Him.

Minbar Is a pulpit in the mosque where the imam stands to deliver sermons.

Qurbani Urdu/ Persian word which literally means an act performed to seek God's pleasure. It is technically used for the sacrifice of an animal slaughtered for the sake of God.

Qur'an A sacred book for muslims, who believe that the Qur'an is the very word of God revealed to Prophet Muhammad. The Qur'an is the principle source of every Muslim's faith and practice. It deals with all subjects that concern us as human beings, including wisdom, doctrine, worship and law; but its basic theme is the relationship between God and His creatures.

Sabr Islamic virtue of 'patience'.

Salah Arabic word for 'prayer' specifically the five daily prayers.

Surah Al-Fatiha 'Surah' is the arabic word for a chapter in the Qur'an (sacred book) of which there are 114 in total. 'Al-Fatiha' is the name of one of those surahs. Muslims believe the Qur'an to have healing properties when recited.

Tahajjud Also known as the "night prayer" is a voluntary prayer, performed by followers of Islam. It is not one of the five obligatory prayers required of all Muslims.

Ummi Arabic/urdu term used for 'mother'.

Wa'alaykum As-salam Used in reply to the greeting of another muslim meaning; peace be upon you.

Ya Allah 'O God'. This phrase is uttered when praying in supplication to God.

Zuhr One of the five daily prayers; the midday prayer.